PRAISE FOR DOLPHIN DUO

"I couldn't wait for this second book of the Dolphin Trainer Mysteries, and wow is it ever as fantastic as I expected and then some! It's a phenomenal mystery with lots of surprise plot twists and yet, it's filled with the Tracey Williams' most beloved strengths as an author – her heart-warming family bonds, her love of animals (this time dolphins and a dove) and her deep connection with worlds beyond Earth and the truths of the life of an empath. Can't wait for the next book in this series!"
--- D. D. Scott, International Bestselling Author

Dolphin Duo

(Dolphin Trainer Mysteries #2)

by

Tracey V. Williams

First Electronic Edition: July 2019

First Print Edition: September 2019

eBook & Print book design & formatting by
D. D. Scott's LetLoveGlow Author Services

Cover Art by Tracey V. Williams

For Mark, with gratitude, for all you have done to help make my writing dreams come true.

For Tweety, the real collared dove, whose joyous spirit and larger-than-life personality inspired me to tell the story this way.

Chloe Martin loves dolphins, her dog Gabe and now…a collared dove.

She's a Senior Trainer at Dolphin Connection, a Southern Florida marine mammal facility. And she's very pregnant with twins. But when the dead body of the facility's dorm manager is discovered, Chloe's past as an amateur sleuth once again becomes very much a part of her present, despite the warnings from the handsome detective assigned to the case, who's now her husband, that it's not safe for her or their unborn twins to pursue her suspicions.

In this YA Mystery, the second in the Dolphin Trainer Mystery Series, there's a murder to solve, lots of dolphins, a sweet dog to love, a rescued collared dove and a romance that fairytales are made of that includes twins on the way. With a beautiful Christian and spiritual element, it also delivers life lessons on faith, unconditional love, the life of an empath with special gifts, and it explores the deep bond that sisters – especially twin sisters – share.

Table of Contents

Twin Duet
(a Dolphin Duo Poem)

Two by two you came to us with style and grace,
If only we could now keep up with your energetic pace.

Your silly giggles fill our home with so much love,
We know you both have been sent directly from heaven
above.

You look at each other with endless understanding and
kindness,
It's hard to believe such little ones could be born with so
much mindfulness.

Always beside you on life's challenging path,
You will find your sister, your other half, just do the math.

Double the adventure, double the fun,
Together you keep your Mommy and Daddy on the run.

Each unique and special in your own way,
You protect each other fiercely and make sure that the
other always has her say.

Being fraternal twins you each have your own look,
But you appear almost the same when you have your nose
in a book.

Partners in life, partners in crime,
Sensitive, sweet and usually on time.

Sunshine and rainbows are clearly down the road,
For being a twin, you have someone with whom to share
life's load.

You will help those who need you with your generous
touch,
Your strength and courage will help many who need you so
much.

Your love and kindness will stretch to levels only a dolphin
can understand,
You will never place on any of your marine counterparts an
unreasonable demand.

Climb high and soar together wherever your roads may
lead,
Knowing having a twin you'll never be in need.

--- *Tracey V. Williams*

Chapter 1

The sun was setting on another beautiful day in southern Florida, and Chloe Martin treasured tender moments like this with her dolphin family. She was still able to get down on the docks and in the water with her marine friends, but she knew it wouldn't be too long before her growing belly would make it really difficult.

It was September now, but it was still hot. Chloe had sweat her way through the summer and spent as much time in the shade as possible.

With a tinge of sadness, she finished up her session with Cali, Emma, Alexa and Sophie. The calves were very independent now and fully involved in the training sessions. She explained to them that she was heading out of town on a trip and would be back in a week.

She was excited to be able to take one last trip before the babies were born. Life had been so busy since she and Brian were married that they hadn't had the chance to get away together other than their honeymoon. They were heading to Colonial Williamsburg, and Chloe couldn't be more excited. It had been some time since she had been to Virginia, and she looked forward to soaking in the history and the scenery.

She gave the girls some last hugs and backrubs and reluctantly left their docks. As she walked to the fish house to clean their coolers, she felt pulled between opposing emotions. Part of her was excited to be going on an adventure with her wonderful husband, but the other part of her was sad that she would be apart from her dolphin family and her sweet dog Gabe for the next week. Every time she was about to take a trip, she struggled with these feelings, but usually felt much better once she had reached her intended destination.

She finished washing the coolers and bid farewell to the two volunteers who were left in the fish house. Even though it was just past closing time, the grounds at Dolphin Connection were eerily empty. Chloe wondered where everyone had disappeared to so quickly.

She popped into the trainer's office and noticed a note taped to her backpack. It was from Rose, a dolphin handler and dear friend who was one of the managers at the dorm where students lived when they came to study at Dolphin Connection. She wanted Chloe to stop by the dorm on her way out that evening. Evidently, she had some things she wanted to give her before she left on vacation.

Since it was after hours, Chloe would drive to the dorm. That way, she could quickly take off for home when she was done.

There were still a lot of cars in the parking lot, which was strange since the grounds had seemed so quiet. Chloe shook her head, too tired to figure it out and awkwardly maneuvered her large belly behind the wheel of her car.

She shifted in her seat and attempted to get comfortable, though her effort outweighed the reward. There wasn't much chance of getting in a better position than she already had herself in, so she decided to get going.

She parked her Mustang as close to the front door as possible which she knew Rose wouldn't mind since she was only stopping by briefly. She shifted and eased herself out from behind the steering wheel which was even harder than getting in. It wouldn't be long before she'd have to trade in her beloved sports car for a family-friendly minivan.

Grabbing her backpack, she locked the car and made her way to the front door. She was eager to get home and make sure everything was ready for their big trip and spend as much time as possible with Gabe. Certainly, he'd try and sneak his way into their luggage. He knew suitcases meant a trip, and he would try his best to go along. Fortunately, he didn't have to board at a kennel while they were gone. Ann and Greg, her beloved friends and owners of the popular Bagels on Broadway, would be keeping him at their house.

As she walked, rather waddled, to the door, she felt a frenetic energy around her. She couldn't quite put her finger on it, but it felt a lot like excitement. She shrugged it off as her own excitement about the trip she and Brian were embarking on in the morning and rang the doorbell at the dorm. She didn't have to wait but a moment before the door swung open and Rose appeared with a broad smile on her face.

"Chloe, come on in my dear! We've... I mean I... have been expecting you."

Chloe stepped inside and received the surprise of her life. Everyone she loved in the world was at the dorm! For a moment, she was speechless, but she recovered quickly. Her family, friends and colleagues had filled the dorm to capacity, joy and enthusiasm coursing throughout the building.

Seeing the shock on her face, Brian rushed to her side and helped steady his pregnant wife before she lost her balance.

"What an amazing surprise, everyone," Chloe said, finally coming to her senses. "Thank you, all of you, for coming together to celebrate our upcoming arrivals. By the looks of it, you all are going to have us prepared times two! That's a lot of gifts!"

She couldn't get over the piles and piles of baby gifts that had been assembled in the presentation room of the dorm. "What a treat for both of us," she continued, smiling over at Brian.

"Who put this whole thing together?" She asked him as he guided her further inside through the scores of people.

"You'll have to ask Rose," he said.

"It was all Theresa," Rose responded. "She got everyone to work together to make this a special evening for you and Brian."

At this point, Chloe had steadied herself enough to start to mingle on her own. She received a giant hug from her twin sister Grace who she was especially surprised to see. Grace immediately informed her that she, Matt and the kids would be joining them on the trip to Williamsburg. Chloe was blown away by the news and squealed in delight.

The rest of the evening flew by. Everyone ate, laughed and reminisced. There were more baby gifts than Chloe knew what to do with and, of course, many of them were dolphin-themed. From onesies to socks to bibs and infant toys – everything seemed to be decorated with a dolphin or two.

Brian even surprised her with a necklace adorned with a charm that had two dolphin calves positioned in such a way as to make a heart. He told her it was symbolic of the deep bond and mutual love their twins would share, just like she and Grace had since the day they were born. Chloe immediately put it on and declared it her favorite.

Rose outdid herself with the food. From pigs-in-a-blanket to oysters-on-the half-shell, she covered it all. She had a way of bringing together many different eclectic tastes to please all palettes. The pasta station and build-your-own taco stand proved to be the winners of the night and were constantly busy. Drinks were served in cups picturing dolphins diving across the beautiful blue ocean, and the non-alcoholic drink of the night was named "The Dolphin Duo." It had mango, pineapple and orange juice blended together into a delicious concoction.

Chloe's favorite food pick of the evening was the dessert. Cannolis, fruit cups and gorgeous chocolates were displayed on a table created just to feature dessert, and it sparkled! And then...there was the cake...

There was an amazing cake that had been created by the owners of a local shop. It featured two, 3-D dolphins diving through waves sculpted out of sugar glass. Each dolphin had a baby bottle to represent the twins on their way. It was such a beautiful work of art, Chloe was sad to have to cut into it. Needless to say, before she made the first slice, many pictures were taken.

As everyone mingled and ate, they also took time to each decorate two onesies (one for each twin), with fabric markers. The final products were hung on a clothesline, the adorable creations proudly displayed. Chloe couldn't wait to dress the twins in each and every set of onesies made by their incredible friends and family. The thoughtfulness that went into each of the designs reminded her of how much she and Brian were loved, and just how much their twins would be, too.

Each of the guests had also written out a special message for both of the twins in a "Wish Book" Chloe's friend Bailey had created. She had written a poem for the babies called "The Dolphin Duo" which was at the front of the book, and then she'd filled the inside with pages decorated with marine mammals where each guest could write their special something. Chloe and Brian knew immediately that the book would be treasured by the twins when they could read it themselves someday. And until then, Chloe and Brian would read it to them often.

Before the party wound down, Chloe caught up with Theresa, her friend and business partner at Dolphin Connection, and expressed her deep gratitude for the event. They were closer than ever, and Chloe knew it meant a lot to her to be able to throw the party. Though the words were never spoken, Chloe knew Theresa desperately missed the companionship of her sister. Having been found guilty, Shannon was serving a life sentence for the murder of Dolphin Connection Researcher Molly Green.

She noticed Brian signal that it was time to go and didn't want to hold things up any longer. She gave Theresa a final hug and bid her goodnight.

As she walked through the kitchen on her way to the back door, Chloe stopped and hesitated in front of the storage freezer. A strange feeling of foreboding washed over her body. She shook off chills that ran from the top of her head right down through her toes.

She sensed something sinister happening in the room, but how could that be?

The dorm kitchen was a communal place where meals were lovingly prepared for students from around the world.

Chloe attributed the dark premonition to her own concern over leaving on a road trip so late in her pregnancy. She hurriedly exited the kitchen to try and change the energy surrounding her.

Chapter 2

"Wake up, everyone!" Brian said and cheered after their morning alarm went off. "It's time to step back into colonial times."

"It can't be 6 AM already," Chloe groaned as she rolled over in bed.

"It most certainly is," Brian announced as he eagerly got ready to shower and change for the day.

"I can't believe how late we were up," Chloe moaned, attempting to squeeze in a few more minutes of sleep before their vacation week started in earnest.

Brian walked over, sat on their bed and gently leaned over and kissed his tired, pregnant wife.

"I'm sorry we were up so late trying to wrangle all the gifts together and cart them home."

"No worries," Chloe said as she turned and faced her doting husband. "The party was awesome, and all of the baby gifts are absolutely amazing – times two! Thank you so much for your part in everything and for having the guest room set up for Grace, Matt and the kids. I still can't believe you were able to pull off that surprise! Wow!"

"Pretty neat, huh? We're going to have so much fun going on vacation together. You and Grace don't get to spend enough time together anymore. This should be a great bonding experience."

"For sure! And to get the time with the kids, too, is such a treat. It should help get me ready for what lies ahead!"

"I thought Grace might help you feel more at ease with what to expect. I know she didn't have twins, but she did have two babies just a few years apart!"

"She is such a competent mom. Parenting looks easy when she does it, but I know that's not the case! I'm going to bring a journal along on the trip, and gently bug her to give me helpful pointers and advice. I'll be like the Dolphin Learner students when they bombard me with all their anxious questions!"

"That's true! You're going to be the one doing the learning this time! From teacher to student in the blink of an eye!"

"Very true. I hope I'm as patient a student as I am a teacher."

"I don't know about that!" Brian chuckled.

"What's that supposed to mean?" Chloe retorted.

"Well, how can I say this nicely? You like to be capable and competent, and when you are concerned you don't know how to do something, you get a little frustrated."

"I do, huh?" Chloe shot back.

"Did I tell you there was one more surprise left before we leave for Virginia?" Brian asked, attempting to change the topic of conversation. "It's a surprise you're going to love!"

"Nice move, changing the topic. Now tell me the surprise before I burst."

"Well, before we hit the road, we are going to make a very special stop this morning at Dolphin Connection. Your niece and nephew have never met your dolphin family in person, and I thought it was high time they had the opportunity. Theresa and I arranged it so that you are on the schedule this morning with your favorite girls. So, let's get you rolled out of this bed!"

"That is like the best surprise ever! I'm so excited to introduce the kids to Alexa, Cali, Emma and Sophie and to see my dolphins one more time before we leave for the week. Help me out of bed, please – I feel like a beached whale!"

"You go shower while I take Gabe for a walk and make sure everyone else is up," Brian instructed as he carefully helped her, knowing how uncomfortable and unsteady she was trying to get out of their bed.

Chloe reassured him she was fine, and he grabbed Gabe while she headed for the shower. She needed to get herself ready so she could get breakfast prepared for their house guests.

Once cleaned up and dressed casually for their road trip, she made her way downstairs to the kitchen where she found Grace, who had already prepared a full spread of scrambled eggs, bacon and toast along with fresh orange juice.

"Grace, you shouldn't have!" Chloe blurted out as she rounded the corner into the kitchen. "What a beautiful sight for this swollen and weary pregnant soul. I'm so tired I wasn't sure how I was going to pull a meal together for all of us!"

"That's the benefit of having a twin – someone who is in perfect sync with you and knows what you need before you even know," Grace said.

"I couldn't imagine going through life without my other half! We are so lucky to be each other's soulmates. Everybody should have a twin – it sure makes getting through this crazy world we live in a little more manageable."

"Couldn't have said it better myself, Sissy. We've been reading each other's minds as long as I can remember. And by the way, I believe that right now, you're thinking we should stop talking and sit down and eat."

"You got that right, for sure!" Chloe exclaimed as she sat down at the kitchen table and began to enjoy the beautiful feast Grace had skillfully prepared.

Matt and the kids joined them a few minutes later and then Gabe pulled Brian to the table when they returned from their walk, not even stopping so Brian could unhook his leash.

Chapter 3

Thanks to Grace, a wonderful breakfast was enjoyed by all, but then chaos descended upon the White household, everyone rushing around in great excitement and preparation to get out of the house and hit the road.

Chloe made sure that Gabe's travel bag was set right by the door so Ann and Greg wouldn't miss it when they stopped by later that day to pick up their poodle houseguest. As good as Gabe was, the bagel store was too crowded and frenzied for him to be dropped off there.

Chloe and Brian would be traveling in his Jeep, and it was packed and ready to go. Grace and her family were set in Chloe's old Jeep, which they would be driving to Williamsburg and then home to Connecticut for an extra vehicle that would be perfect for toting Jackson's hockey equipment to and from practice.

Chloe had kept the Jeep in addition to her Mustang so that she could drive it to work on occasions when she was in the water a great deal and when she went on dolphin and manatee strandings. After those outings, she often was pretty messy, and she could easily throw her wet stuff into the older vehicle with no worries.

With the babies on the way, her stranding days were over for now. Since she had no more use for the sturdy Jeep, she was happy to pass it onto Grace. Brian had convinced her that it wouldn't do for twins, and that a minivan was the only way to go when she finally traded in her Mustang.

Since Grace and Matt planned to take an extra week after their stay in Williamsburg, slowly making their way back to Connecticut, it all worked out well. They planned to stop in Washington, D.C. and the Jersey Shore.

Chloe couldn't wait until she and Brian were taking their own adventures with their twins.

The whole family headed over to Dolphin Connection, with Chloe and Brian leading the way. Chloe wiped the tears that had formed from the corners of her eyes as she thought about how sad Gabe was to see them leave.

"He'll be fine, and you know it," Brian reminded her. "He's always upset when we first leave, and then he has a great time with Ann and Greg. You know they spoil him rotten!"

"I know, I know. He'll be happily content during our absence, but I still feel like a louse for leaving him. It never gets easier, and I'm afraid it's going to be even harder with the twins! I don't think you'll be able to tear me away from them!"

"I can only imagine…" Brian mumbled quietly, almost to himself.

"Here we are!" Chloe piped up, thrilled they were almost to Dolphin Connection, the perfect reprieve from her worries.

As the words rolled off her lips, she felt a blast of frosty air shoot through the car and a sense that someone she loved was cold…very cold.

"Did you sense that wave of chilly air, or is it just me?" Chloe asked Brian.

"It's just the air conditioning. I had it turned way up to cool off the car this morning."

"No, this was different. The AC has been on since we left the house. This chilly air had a dark vibe to it. Something isn't right, but I have no clue what. I wish I could more fully understand these snippets of information I'm sent from the other side."

"Chloe, please, that's ridiculous. Let it go. Right now, we're here on this side heading in for a dolphin swim with your adorable niece and nephew. Enjoy the moment. No need to make something out of nothing."

"I most certainly will cherish this wonderful opportunity to introduce Jackson and Kristen to their dolphin relatives, but I won't let this go. Something is off, I'm just not sure what. Mark my words, a case is just around the corner."

"Please don't say that," Brian pleaded. "We're trying to leave on vacation. A well-deserved adventure before the twins are born. We both work hard, and we need this break."

"You couldn't be more right, but some things are out of our control. For now, I'll push it to the side. And since the kids are waving furiously for us to get out of the car and get them to the dolphins, it looks like I'll have to. They are just the distraction I need. Come on, slow poke, let's do this!"

Chloe turned and smiled at her bewildered husband, knowing he still found himself befuddled at times by the way in which she could so smoothly glide between emotions.

Chapter 4

"Come on, everyone! We have an amazing marine interaction planned for y'all!" Chloe escorted Brian, Grace, Matt, Kristen and Jackson through the gift shop and straight to her office.

Since she had been promoted to Vice President of Operations, she enjoyed a private office. Though she missed the comradery of the trainer's office, it had been very helpful to have some extra privacy during the pregnancy and on days like today when she was entertaining family.

She had everyone drop off their bags in her office, and they emerged with their towels, flip flops and not much else. She had them leave behind sunglasses, hats and any other loose items that could fall into the dolphins' lagoon.

"This way, this way!" She practically cheered as she brought her family into the trainer's office to make sure they were still on with her favorite girls. Everyone knew Brian, of course, and had met Grace, Matt and the kids back at their wedding as well as at the shower the night before.

Chloe checked the schedule board for last minute changes. All looked the same as the one she'd received by email. Theresa had finally stepped into modern times and stopped faxing the schedule in addition to emailing it.

Personally, Chloe also thought the fax machine was a reminder of what happened the night Molly Green was murdered and understood why Theresa had removed it from the building immediately following Shannon's trial.

Bailey, a senior dolphin trainer and Chloe's close friend, came around the corner and gave her and her entourage a warm greeting.

"Why don't I join you all so that you can really savor the time with your family, Chloe?" Bailey offered.

"That sounds terrific! Thanks for the offer, Bailey. Let's bring them all over to the fish house and pick up the coolers for the girls."

They escorted their excited group over to the fish house and had each of them wash their feet in the foot bath before they entered. The kids were interested to learn this kept germs from being carried into the fish house on the bottom of their feet. They learned it was important to keep everything sanitary for the dolphins in order to keep them healthy. What they didn't understand was why it smelled so bad in the fish house.

"It stinks in here!" Jackson blurted out.

"It's like someone sprayed a can of fish odor fragrance throughout the room," Grace agreed.

"After a few days, you get used to it," Bailey offered.

The volunteers in the fish house nodded in agreement.

"And you get used to picking fish scales off your arms and hands on a regular basis," Chloe chimed in.

"That sounds stinky and gross!" Jackson erupted.

"But worth it to have the amazing opportunity to work with the dolphins," Chloe informed him.

"I do hope I find a job someday that I love as much as you love yours, Aunt Chloe," Jackson commented, sounding much more mature than his seven years of age.

"I hope you do too, sweetheart. It is truly a blessing to love what you do," Chloe shared as she gave her nephew a quick squeeze and smiled at him.

She just couldn't wait to have these moments with her own children, and the wait wouldn't be much longer now.

As they all left the fish house carrying the girls' coolers and headed to the front lagoon for their swim, the kids couldn't be more excited.

Chloe led the way and guided her overjoyed niece and nephew down to the floating dock, carefully steadying herself as she did so. The memory of the first time Brian stepped onto the dock and almost fell in the water was never far from her thoughts.

The girls popped right up, all four of them, completely surprising Kristen and Jackson. They giggled with delight which excited the dolphins immensely, prompting them to make giggly noises themselves.

The wide range of noises dolphins can make, including loud raspberries, fascinated the kids. They didn't know dolphins could squeak, chirp, whistle, click and make raspberry sounds.

Chloe was overjoyed by their fascination, and the warmth being shared by her adorable dolphins and her equally adorable niece and nephew made her heart grow with pride.

As she joined in the music-making session by giving the dolphins signals for every noise they could make, they all laughed. Her belly was so large now it jiggled like that of Santa Claus, which made them laugh even harder.

Chloe noticed Brian beaming as he watched her in her element, on the docks with the dolphins. It meant everything to her that he paid attention to what made her happy and shared in those joys with her, as she knew he would with their children.

"Okay, everyone, let's get this swim party started! We could be here all day soaking in all these beautiful vocals, but I can't wait to get you all in the water with these amazing girls. Leave your flip flops, shirts and towels up on the pier and carefully step down onto the floating dock. Take it slow, Matt and Grace, so that you don't lose your balance. Brian almost fell in the first time he stepped down here," Chloe heartily added.

"Thanks for sharing that embarrassing tidbit with the rest of the family, sweetheart!" Brian chided with a look letting her know he wasn't really mad at her.

Chloe was forever offering TMI. And receiving it. Speaking of which, she suddenly had the strangest feeling that something terrible had happened that would rock Dolphin Connection to its core, once again. She had sort of blown off – okay, she'd tried to without much success – her premonition the previous night in the dorm kitchen and then the cold blast in the car on the way to Dolphin Connection, but now she wondered if she shouldn't have and that these multiple rushes of information and dreadful feelings were somehow connected.

"Make room for Mommy, Daddy and Uncle Brian," Kristen announced, sounding more like she was 40 than 4. The young child's request quickly brought Chloe back to the present moment as she moved out of the way to make room for the other adults.

Chapter 5

As soon as everyone had successfully assembled on the floating dock, Chloe had them kneel at its edge on either side of her. Jackson and Brian were on her right and Kristen, Grace and Matt were on her left. Bailey went ahead and entered the water to be alongside the dolphins so she could assist from that position.

All four of the girls were so excited to see Chloe with her loved ones she didn't even have to call them over to the dock, they were already there and waiting. Their captivating faces made it easy for her to move on from the ominous feelings she had been experiencing.

"Now everyone carefully place one hand, palm down, on the surface of the water, and I'll have each of the girls come by for a backrub. You can start your backrub below the blowhole and give a nice rub up and down each dolphin's back! I can't wait to hear what you think the dolphins feel like," Chloe said as she turned and smiled at Jackson and then Kristen. "The first dolphin you are going to meet is Cali – she is the mom to these awesome twins and a great example of a loving, doting mother."

Chloe signaled Cali and the responsive dolphin swam next to the dock so that everybody had a chance to greet her with affectionate back rubs. The kids each squealed in delight as neither of them had touched a dolphin before this moment.

"She' so soft and squishy!" Jackson shouted excitedly.

"I can't believe I'm touching a real dolphin, Auntie," Kristen squawked as she turned and gave Chloe a huge grin.

"I remember my first dolphin interaction like it was yesterday," Chloe said to her sweet niece. "It was one of the most special moments of my life, and I knew I was right where I belonged. I would have been happy to work with any marine mammals, but Atlantic Bottlenose Dolphins like these girls have a special place in my heart because they were the first marine mammals I learned about in school and subsequently met in person. They are the species that most people are familiar with from books, shows and movies. They captured my heart at first sight."

"Let's meet another dolphin please, Aunt Chloe," Kristen begged enthusiastically.

"Yes, let's meet another beautiful dolphin!" Chloe agreed. "We are going to greet a very special, mature female dolphin named Emma – she is fortunate to be an aunt just like me. She never had calves of her own, but luckily, she treats Alexa and Sophie like they are her calves."

"Does that bother Cali?" Grace questioned.

"Not at all. Being a dolphin mother, as being a human mother, is a full-time job, and Cali seems to simply appreciate the help. Since mature male and female dolphins only come together for mating purposes and do not live together as a family unit, the other females in a maternity pod naturally support the pregnant females, nursing mothers and newborn calves."

"That makes sense to me," Grace responded, being a tired mother of two energetic youngsters herself. "Though it seems sad to think that the male dolphins don't help nurture their young. Would the father of a calf even recognize it in the wild?"

"Great question, Sis! Dolphins have a signature whistle which helps identify each individual dolphin. Researchers think the whistle helps male dolphins identify their offspring, so they do not mate with them when they are sexually mature. Sort of nature's way of keeping things healthy amongst the dolphin population."

"Interesting! There is so much to learn about these intelligent beauties!" Grace noted.

"Sure, Mom, but remember we're on vacation from school!" Jackson offered.

"That's true," Chloe agreed, always the sympathetic aunt. "Learning is fun, too though, but today our focus is interaction. So, let's keep going. Emma, it's your turn."

Chloe kept eye contact with Emma as she signaled her to come to the dock. Emma stayed extra-long for her rubs as she thoroughly enjoyed human contact.

Finally, Chloe, with a short, high-pitched whistle blow, bridged Emma, indicating to her that the behavior was finished, and it was time for a fish reward. Emma was glad to receive a handful of sardines – the kids were still getting used to the idea of the "fish for food" thing and squealed in disgust each time Chloe opened a cooler and pulled out a handful of stinky, slimy fish.

"You two are going to have to come live with me one summer when you are both old enough to volunteer in the fish house. That will get you over the fish thing for sure!"

"No, no, please don't make us, Auntie!" Jackson and Kristen both pleaded.

"I don't know, guys, I think it would be good for you, too!" Their Dad joked.

"Stop tormenting the children," Brian interjected and received grateful smiles from his niece and nephew-in-law.

"Good way to earn brownie points with the little ones, Mr. White," Chloe said to her husband. "Should I expect the same when we have our own children?"

"For sure!" Brian said. "Children should always think their father is the center of the universe."

"That's fine, as long as they think their mother is, too!" Chloe responded in kind, her heart brimming with anticipation and hopefulness that their children would feel that way once they were in the world and had experienced their joy and love-filled parenting.

The kids quickly forgave Chloe as they, in turn, gave backrubs to Alexa and Sophie. Jackson and Kristen could relate to the smaller size of the young calves since they were indeed smaller themselves.

"They are so cute, Auntie," Kristen screeched. "I absolutely love their pink bellies! How come they have much pinker bellies than Cali and Emma?" She asked with enthusiasm.

"Dolphin calves are born with varying degrees of pinkish tummies and then the pink tends to fade as they grow and mature. Of course, some fade more than others. Since Alexa and Sophie are still calves, they continue to have the pinkish hue on their belly region. Time will tell how much it will stay or fade for each of them. It's sort of like how some humans have blond hair when they are born and then it darkens to more of a light brown color," Chloe explained.

"That happened to your hair, Kristen. Your eyes changed from blue to green in your first year, too!" Grace noted.

"They did?" The child asked in disbelief.

"Yes, they surely did," her Mom responded.

"I think I'd like my blond hair and blue eyes back, thank you," Kristen politely demanded.

"It doesn't work that way, sweetheart," Grace explained to her perplexed child. "You just can't change the color of your hair and eyes."

"Not until you get older and can get your hair colored and wear special contacts!" Matt joked.

"That is true," Grace agreed, "But nothing Kristen needs to worry about for a long time," she said to her young daughter as she shot her husband an irritated glance. "You are perfect just the way you are, Kristen!"

"That's very true," Chloe chimed in. "You are unique, Kristen – perfectly yourself as you grow and mature in God's image. Just like Alexa and Sophie will be even if their tummies fade from pink to grey. We'll love them and think they are beautiful just the same."

"I know you'll love them just the same, Auntie," Kristen added. "But, I really do love their pink bellies – they are so adorable, and pink is my favorite color."

"Enough girl talk," Jackson interjected, with the support of his father and uncle. "I want to get in and swim with the dolphins. I can't wait any longer – I'm just too excited for words!"

"Jackson, I couldn't agree with you more," Chloe responded. "It's that special time when you all get to slip into the water and swim with the dolphins. I'm going to have you all carefully slide into the water and hang onto the dock so that you can clearly hear me give you directions. Bailey will stay in the water and assist from there, and I'll stay here on the dock. This growing belly is making it a little difficult for me to get out of the water lately, and I don't want to push it too hard before we hit the road for our trip."

"No worries, Chloe!" Bailey exclaimed from the water with a big smile on her face. "You know this is my favorite place in the world – I'd stay in here all day with these beautiful girls if I could!"

"It is my happy place, as well. I miss being able to easily get in and out of the water. It's worth it, though, to have the exceptional opportunity to carry these two around for nine months," Chloe said as she rubbed her swollen belly.

"Very worth it!" Grace verified from personal experience.

After sharing a warm smile with her wonderful sister, Chloe gave the four dolphins in the maternity pod the signal for front dives, and they all took off together. Simultaneously, the excited group of swimmers made their way safely into the water.

Being that the water was about 85 degrees Fahrenheit, it wasn't too difficult for any of them to slip into the water without fanfare. Once everyone was in the water and holding onto the dock, Chloe blew her whistle to bridge the dolphins. They finished their last front dives and sped back to the dock for a fish snack.

Bailey signaled for the calves to come over to her using the symbols that she had brought into the water. Each dolphin at the facility had been trained to recognize and respond to a unique symbol that was assigned to him or her, like a circle or a square. As each one touched her snout, or rostrum, to her symbol, Bailey bridged them and gave them hugs and kisses as their reward. She kept them busy, while Chloe had the more mature Cali and Emma handle the first in-water interaction with her family.

Each participant had the opportunity to choose a certain behavior such as splashing or spinning in a circle and having the dolphins imitate them. Kristen couldn't get enough of the splashing, and Jackson boldly chose spitting water. He quickly learned the two dolphins were able to generate a lot more water with their long rostrums than he was capable with his small, human mouth.

Hugs and kisses followed, and then everyone had the opportunity to be pushed around the lagoons while resting on their backs. All they had to do was float and enjoy being pushed as the dolphins pressed their rostrums into the bottom of each participant's feet.

Of course, Chloe left the grand finale for the completion of the swim. When they heard the news that they would each get a dorsal pull from the calves, and have the opportunity to speed around the lagoon being pulled by a dolphin, Kristen and Jackson were thrilled beyond belief.

"It's your time to shine, baby girls!" Chloe called over to the two enthusiastic dolphin calves who were starting to get impatient. "Let's swap dolphins, Bailey."

The task was accomplished with ease. Cali and Emma were soon relaxing with Bailey while Alexa and Sophie were waiting anxiously at the front of the dock for a signal. Chloe explained to each of her family members that one-by-one they would swim to the middle of the lagoon and wait for the calves to pop up and meet them. Then, they would reach out on both sides and hold onto the dorsal fin of each dolphin.

"Get ready to hold on tight!" Chloe called to Jackson as he treaded water a good distance from the dock. He desperately wanted to go first, and his cooperative sister didn't object.

"I'm ready to go, Aunt Chloe," Jackson called out.

Chloe gave Alexa and Sophie the appropriate signal, and they both sped out to Jackson and quickly popped up on either side of him.

When the dolphins appeared, Jackson's look of surprise was priceless. He immediately reached out and seamlessly grabbed hold of the dorsal fins on his sides. The smile on his face was not overshadowed by the squeals of delight he let loose as the energetic calves took him for the ride of his life with three laps around the lagoon.

Chloe finally bridged the girls, and they ducked under the water and zoomed back to the dock where they popped up screeching and waiting for their delicious herring!

"Awesome job, girls!" Chloe praised the young calves with excitement equal to theirs. "Swim on back to the dock yourself, Jackson, and we'll have Kristen take her turn."

"Could they go a little slower for me please, Aunt Chloe?" Kristen asked.

"Absolutely, honey. You go ahead and swim into place, and I'll settle the girls down. You'll be amazed at how gentle they can be when they know that is what the individual needs. They just took Jackson for a wild ride because that is what he wanted! Dolphins are amazing at reading a person's energy," Chloe explained. "They'll tailor the swim to your needs, so just relax and enjoy it. You're in good flippers, Kristen."

With that knowledge, Kristen confidently doggy paddled a few feet from the dock and smiled as Sophie and Alexa gently and gracefully appeared on both sides of her. Never astonished by the depth of intelligence her marine sisters bestowed, Chloe simply smiled inwardly as she watched the calves take Kristen for a dorsal ride that was perfectly suited for her very young age and small size.

Of course, the calves had no trouble going back into full gear for Matt and Brian – amazing the two grown men with their strength and style. For Grace, well, they were graceful, and that suited her just fine!

"Okay, everyone! Sadly, it's time to wrap-up our in-water time with these beautiful girls. If everyone, including you Bailey, wants to come back up on the dock, we could spend a few more minutes interacting with the pod by playing with some of their toys."

Chloe hoped that last offer would help ease the kids out of the water and onto the dock. She knew personally how difficult it was for such an exciting experience to come to a close, so she thought offering a transition activity might help to bring things to an easier end.

It worked! Both Kristen and Jackson cooperatively pushed themselves up out of the water and onto the dock with an ease that was natural for children and immediately started to toss a couple of the girls' favorite balls and hula hoops into the water.

"Look, Auntie, look!" Kristen shouted excitedly as Cali adeptly hooked each of her pectoral fins underneath a hula hoop and started dragging them around the lagoon.

"Look over here," Jackson countered, not to be outdone by his younger sister. He demonstrated a game of ball he was playing with Emma.

"She's bopping the ball right back to you with her rostrum, Jackson!" Chloe exclaimed. "I'll bet that's the best game of ball you've ever played!"

"It is, it is!" He agreed as he continued to thoroughly enjoy throwing the ball to Emma and having it immediately returned to him.

As Chloe and Bailey were helping the kids on the dock, Matt, Grace and Brian toweled off and slipped on their flip flops so they would be ready to go.

"I certainly don't want to rush you, Dolphin Girl, but the day is swimming by! We should probably get a move on if we're still going to start our road trip to Virginia today," Brian gently reminded his wife.

"It is getting late!" Chloe agreed. "And it's time for us to give these four girls some dolphin time! Why don't you help me give them their last fish and show them their empty cooler?" Chloe asked her eager and helpful niece and nephew.

The kids were thrilled to help, and both even got over their fishy trepidations to feed a treat to their new best friends. By letting them see the inside of each cooler and then pouring the leftover ice into the water, they loved showing the dolphins that the session was over.

"That's a great idea!" Jackson commented. "You can see how they understand the session is over when the fish are gone. It really works!"

"Yes, it does!" Chloe agreed. "It's simple and clear and done in the same way every time. Animals appreciate consistency, just like humans."

As Chloe was praising the kids and the dolphins for such a great session, the spirit of joy that had surrounded them was suddenly permeated by a blood-curdling scream.

Chapter 6

Chloe and the kids were so startled by the alarming scream they jumped to their feet, at least the kids jumped – Chloe struggled and set the floating dock into convulsions. She grabbed Kristen just before she went flying back into the lagoon.

Grace and Matt rushed back down onto the dock to safeguard their children, and Brian started running towards the screaming. Vacation or not, his police instincts were always on duty.

"Everyone stay here while I go find out what happened," he shouted over his shoulder.

"Be safe!" Chloe called back as she watched her husband run towards the danger. "I'll never get used to the responsibilities of his job," she blurted out, almost apologetically.

"Very understandable," Grace assured her as she wrapped her arms around her pregnant twin sister. "I'm sure it's especially scary now that you all are starting a family."

"I'm feeling the anxiety more than ever the closer my due date creeps. I'm so proud of all that Brian has accomplished in his professional life and feel the gratitude from all the families he has helped, several just since we met, but sometimes, I wish he had a normal job!"

"Don't fool yourself, Chloe. In this day and age, there aren't any normal jobs left. We all take our lives into our hands every time we head into the world!" Matt joked, obviously trying to lighten up the moment.

"That's very true," Chloe agreed. "Thanks for bringing me back to my senses, Matt! Brian loves his job and seems to have a guardian angel who watches over him and keeps him safe."

"Trust your gut, Chloe. You know Brian is following God's plan for him. He is a natural detective," Matt continued. "His instincts are second to none."

"I agree, and I know he is truly following his calling. I just can't imagine what has happened here at Dolphin Connection today to cause such a commotion and set him off with such a start. Since Molly's murder, we all have prayed for peace and calm throughout these grounds. It doesn't seem possible that this beautiful setting could be the location of another tragedy," Chloe said with much more hopeful conviction than she felt, "though, I have received three unsettling premonitions in the last day about just this."

"Let's not jump to any conclusions," Grace offered as she wrapped her arms back around the kids who were looking up at their Aunt Chloe with bewildered looks.

"Has someone been murdered here?" Jackson questioned timidly after hearing his aunt.

"Oh, honey, there is no need for you to worry about that," Chloe answered, immediately regretting how reckless she'd been speaking of murder in front of her niece and nephew.

It was going to take a little work for her to get used to thinking through everything she said before it came out of her mouth. Having young influential minds around really did change your life.

"I'm sorry, Gracey," Chloe offered to her twin. "I'm not used to having inquiring minds around all the time."

"No worries – they'll be fine. This is good practice for you to start to see just how much your life is about to change," Grace replied. "I'll explain to them in kid terms what happened with the Molly situation."

"Thanks, Gracey. I feel silly for being so ignorant."

"Once again – no worries. Chloe, you are going to be amazed at how much you have to learn once your sweet babies are born. But, I'm not worried. You always pick up things fast. And the lessons will be coming at you…times two!"

"Overwhelming to say the least. Hopefully, Brian and I will be successful at this parenting thing together. It sure sounds like it's going to take both of us being fully committed with twins," she said, unable to hide neither her excitement nor her fear.

"Sounds right to me, Dolphin Girl," Brian interjected as he approached on the boardwalk.

Chloe, Grace, Matt and the kids had been so engrossed in conversation they hadn't heard him coming.

"You surprised us, Brian!" Chloe said, so relieved he was back.

"Stealth mode," he said as he made his way down the steps onto the floating dock.

"Was all the screaming a false alarm?" Chloe asked.

"Unfortunately, it wasn't. There's been an accident. When Rose went looking for Jack this morning, she found him with an ice pick in his chest. She'd been searching for him, and when she discovered his lifeless body, that was her scream we heard."

Chloe was shocked to the point she could barely speak. She felt as if she might faint. Brian quickly supported her back to make sure she didn't drop to the ground.

She couldn't imagine what Rose would do without Jack. Not only was he her faithful husband, he was the backbone of the dorm.

"So, he is dead?" She whispered, almost inaudibly.

Brian nodded, letting her know Jack was indeed gone.

"I don't believe it," Chloe blurted out as she started to sob uncontrollably. She and Jack shared a special friendship. They had since they'd met more than ten years ago. It seemed unimaginable to her that her friend, and the beloved manager of the dorm for the Dolphin Learners (the student-centered programs at Dolphin Connection), could possibly be gone from this world.

"Let's get you back to your office," Brian offered. "You need to get inside the air conditioning and sit down before you pass out on me."

"I'll be okay," Chloe said, noticing that both Jackson and Kristen were watching her.

She had to pull herself together. Clearly, having children around required a person to not only constantly think about what they were saying but also how they reacted to things, even to heart-wrenching news.

"Why are you crying, Aunt Chloe?" Kristen asked in a worried voice.

"I just found out that one of my friends had an accident, and I feel sad for him, honey. Uncle Brian and I are going to check on what happened," she said.

There was no way she would go hide in her office.

"Why don't you, Jackson, Mommy and Daddy have some lunch? They have the best fish and chips at the café and even a key lime milkshake. I know how you love key lime anything!"

"That sounds like a great idea, Chloe," Grace interrupted. "We will swing by your office and get dressed, then head to the café for a delicious lunch. Let's get going, kids!"

"Can we say "hi" to the other dolphins on our way?" Jackson asked. "I want to make sure I meet them all while we are here, you know, to be fair and all."

"That's a great idea, and you know I am in full agreement with you about the fairness thing. Let's let every dolphin know we are here to meet each one of them," Grace offered to her oldest child as she and Matt hurriedly scooped up the kids to set off on their own adventure, getting them as far away from the stressful discussion of the accident as possible.

As they were leaving the dock, Grace hugged Chloe and whispered into her ear with a little too much breath, making it tickle as she had since they were children, "We'll keep the kids distracted while you and Brian gather more information regarding what has occurred over at the dorm. Text me when you know what's going on."

"I'll do just that," Chloe said, with gratitude.

Chapter 7

Chloe gave Brian "the look," and he clearly understood that his stubborn wife was not going to head back to the comfort and safety of her office, so together, they made their way to the dorm.

The coroner was arriving as they were walking up the steps, and it all seemed so surreal, even to Brian, a seasoned detective.

"This can't be happening," Chloe murmured as she and Brian entered the front door and searched for Rose.

"There is Rose in the Seminar Room, Chloe. Why don't you go and sit with her while I go talk to the coroner and start the investigation process," Brian said, more as a suggestion than a question.

Chloe nodded. She understood her role at the scene was to support her good friend, Rose. Brian had made it very clear during Molly's murder investigation that he didn't feel it was appropriate for Chloe to get involved in his work. She was the dolphin trainer. He was the detective.

She headed towards Rose who was sitting alone hunched over in one of the seminar chairs. As she walked across the living room, she noticed the decorations from the previous night's festivities that still adorned the walls. It didn't seem possible that, less than 24 hours earlier, the dorm had been filled with such joy.

Life could be cruel sometimes, offering the extremes of emotions.

Chloe felt herself becoming overwhelmed and immediately tried to rein in her grief before she reached her friend. She was there to comfort, not be comforted.

As she approached Rose, she noticed a strange sense wash over her. Rose was grief-stricken for sure, but she also seemed to be embodying another strong emotion. Chloe could almost taste the guilt emanating from Rose's spirit.

Chapter 8

"Rose, it's me," Chloe gently sobbed as she wrapped her arms around her friend's neck. When she came face to face with Rose's grief, the tears she fought to hold back simply released themselves.

"Chloe, thank you for being here. I thought you were leaving for Virginia this morning," Rose said, clearly confused.

"We were supposed to take off early this morning, but Brian surprised me by setting up a dolphin swim for my sister and her family. We were down on the dock finishing our session when we heard your scream. At least I'm assuming that was you we heard scream," she said, trying to gently encourage Rose to tell her what had happened.

"That was indeed me," Rose confirmed. "I was the one who found Jack. We were up late last night cleaning up from the party, and I slept-in this morning since we don't have any students staying at the dorm this week. When I got out of bed, I noticed Jack's sheets and covers were undisturbed which alarmed me. It appeared as if he had never made it to bed. When we'd said goodnight, I thought he was simply finishing up a few remaining things. I was asleep before my head hit the pillow. I was so tired, I never realized Jack hadn't made it upstairs. I quickly dressed and ran downstairs to try and find out what was going on. I had last seen him in the prep kitchen, and that's where I found him…in front of the walk-in freezer. There was water all over the floor, and he was face down in the middle of it. I rushed to him, turned him over and was shocked to see an ice pick in his chest. That's when I screamed and called 9-1-1."

"Oh, Rose, how horrible! I'm so, so sorry for your loss. It must have been devastating to find him in such a way. What do you think happened?"

"I don't know, Chloe. When I left him, he was using the pick to break up some large blocks of ice that were supporting the ice sculpture of the dolphins. He'd said he wanted to chop up the ice so we could use it for the students that are due to arrive next Friday. He never wanted to waste anything, not even ice, and it was a simple job for a man of his strength and size. When I said goodnight to him, he was about halfway done and had already filled one cooler with ice chips and placed it in the storage freezer. I wish I had stayed to help him finish. If I had insisted on helping him, this never would have happened. But, Chloe, you know Jack. He directed me to go to bed. I was falling asleep on my feet, and he wouldn't stand me working for another minute."

"Rose, this isn't your fault. You had no way of knowing Jack would suffer such a crazy accident. What a fluke. Tired or not, Jack was so sound, so strong. I can't fathom how this could have happened. A terrible, terrible accident. Once again, I'm so sorry, my friend."

"Thank you, Chloe. I'm so relieved you are here, and the dolphins kept you from already being on the road. I don't think I could get through this without you."

"I'm not going anywhere, Rose," Chloe reassured her distraught friend, fully knowing her last hurrah before the twins arrived, or "babymoon" as some called it, had definitely been cancelled.

"What about your trip? You have to go on your trip. Your family will be so disappointed if you don't go," Rose said worriedly.

"They'll understand," Chloe reassured her inconsolable friend.

"Thank you, Chloe. You are a rock, and I need your strength right now. I just feel so guilty and sad all wrapped up in one."

"I'll be your rock, Rose. Though please don't feel guilty. You have nothing to feel guilty about, nothing at all," Chloe reassured her friend.

For some reason, though, Chloe questioned the reassurance she offered. She couldn't seem to clear the air of the guilt that hovered around Rose's aura.

Chapter 9

With a heavy heart, Chloe searched for Grace, Matt and the kids over at the Dolphin Connection Café. When she entered the dining room and scanned the area, Kristen and Jackson waved their arms furiously. Their enthusiasm only made it harder for her to deliver the sad news that she and Brian wouldn't be able to make it for the trip to Williamsburg.

To Chloe's relief, everyone understood immediately. After watching Chloe clutch her stomach and wince in pain, Grace mentioned she even thought it might be for the best.

"Are you okay, Chloe? You look like you're in pain," Grace said as she pulled out a chair for her other half to sit down.

"I'm not sure what that was all about," Chloe responded, gratefully taking a seat. "I just got a sharp pain and tensing feeling in my pelvis."

"That sounds like a Braxton Hicks contraction," Grace replied. "Have you had any up to this point? I don't think you have mentioned any," Grace questioned her sister, the worry obvious in her voice.

"No, this is definitely the first. I'd have remembered to talk to you about something this painful. My doctor said they might start to occur in the third trimester, but it is scary, nonetheless."

"Stay calm and breathe, Chloe. I'll text Brian to come over from the dorm. I'm sure everything will be fine," Grace tried to reassure her.

While Grace tried to get in touch with Brian, Matt retrieved a glass of cold water for Chloe.

"Thanks, Matt," Chloe said as she accepted the water and took a long drink. "I believe I may have overdone it with all the excitement this morning," she said, wincing from another contraction.

"Chloe, why don't we get you to your office? You can lie down on your left side, which places the least amount of pressure on the babies, and try to calm yourself down. We also need to make sure you are properly hydrated after being outside for a couple of hours, so keep drinking that water," Grace suggested.

"Chloe, what's going on, sweetie?" Brian asked as he rushed into the room.

"How did you get here so fast?" She asked her frantic husband.

"I ran. What's going on? Are you okay or should we see Dr. Block?"

"I'm not sure. I've just had a couple of Braxton Hicks contractions. They were spread out and seem to have subsided now that I've drank some water. I'd like to rest on the couch in my office and drink more water before I make a decision about what to do next," she said.

"That sounds like a smart idea," Brian agreed. "If you all are done with lunch, why don't we gather ourselves together in Chloe's office. It will be more private there."

The group quickly cleaned off their table, gathered their belongings and made their way out of the café. Grace and Brian each supported Chloe by an elbow as she walked, and Matt took the hands of Kristen and Jackson.

"Now that I'm comfortably reclined and have rehydrated, I feel a lot better. Thankfully, the contractions seem to have stopped. Though we should still probably check-in with Dr. Block since ours is a high-risk pregnancy."

"Definitely," Brian firmly agreed. "I'll call and see if they can get you in this afternoon. While disappointing that we won't be able to make it to Williamsburg, I'm glad this didn't happen on the road."

"Very true," Grace agreed. "We're going to miss you all on the trip, but I'm relieved that Chloe will be at home close to her doctor. I've had my trepidations about her traveling this late in her pregnancy."

"Home does seem like the place to be at this juncture. Once these babies are born, we'll have an awesome family adventure," Matt added.

"It's a deal. In the meantime, I want you all to send us tons of pictures, so we feel like we're there ourselves," Chloe requested.

"That won't be a problem for Grace. You know how she loves to take way too many pictures," Matt joked.

"Very funny," Grace chimed in. "I'm going to do something extra creative this time, though, and make a photo journal that I'll post each day so that Chloe can follow along," Grace said.

Chloe could see the proverbial wheels spinning as Grace explained what she was simultaneously figuring out in her head.

"That would be thoughtful, Gracey. Thank you. Now, you all need to hit the road before it gets too late in the day," Chloe encouraged, even though there was a huge part of her that wanted them to stay.

"Are you sure you don't want us to stay?" Grace asked Chloe.

"I'm sure. There's no reason for you all to stay here and watch me rest. I'll feel better if I know you are continuing on with our plans. Once I'm feeling rested, I'll be helping Rose with Jack's funeral arrangements and that will keep me plenty busy."

"Please don't hesitate to let us know if you need anything," Grace said.

"Thank you for the offer, but I'm sure I'll be just fine. Brian is quite the doting husband, as we all know. Let me give big hugs before you leave. Kids, come on over here and give your auntie some loving. It will have to last until next time we see each other."

Jackson and Kristen gave Chloe lots of cuddly hugs, kisses and thanks for such a great visit.

"We're going to keep learning about dolphins when we get home," the siblings blurted out, almost in unison.

"That makes me both proud and happy," Chloe said, feeling her heart expand with her niece and nephew's love for her passion and life's work.

After she and Matt said their farewells, Grace was last to go. She laid both her hands on Chloe's tummy and told the twins she'd be back as soon as they were born.

"I know we have to set out on our road trip," she said, "but I never fully leave your side. Part of my heart and my spirit always stays with you."

"And mine with you," Chloe reminded her twin, her gratitude for their connection unable to be fully expressed in words, although they knew it in their hearts and souls.

Had Brian not broken the beauty of the moment with his announcement that Chloe's doctor wanted to see her right away, **their** farewell might have lasted much longer.

Chapter 10

With Grace, Matt and the kids on the road and Chloe receiving a clean bill of health from her doctor, life returned to normal. Well…normal meaning she could continue with normal activity as long as she stayed mostly indoors, drank plenty of fluids and steered clear of any outside stress on her life.

She and Brian picked up an excited Gabe from a very surprised Ann and Greg, then went home to have a relaxing evening.

Since she was already on vacation for the week, she would easily have time to support Rose as she prepared for Jack's funeral. Although, she wasn't sure her doctor would consider that activity stress-free, so she'd simply have to keep it low key and let Brian manage the "heavy lifting."

"Have you heard anything more about Jack's death?" She asked Brian as they both enjoyed the Chinese food they had picked up for dinner.

"Not much yet. Hopefully, once the autopsy is done tomorrow, we'll have more information. Since we're staying home now, they've asked me to take lead on the investigation. Is that okay with you? I can save the week off then for when the babies come."

"That makes sense, and I'm sure Rose will feel better knowing you are heading up the investigation. Was there any evidence of foul play when you first combed the scene this afternoon?"

"Things looked as normal as they could considering the situation, but I need to get back over there tomorrow to follow-up and to interview Rose."

"Why do you need to interview Rose? You don't think she had anything to do with this, do you, Brian?" Chloe worriedly asked her husband, not able to clear the nagging energy of guilt she'd felt around Rose earlier.

"You know it's protocol, Chloe. When there has been an accident, next of kin is always viewed with some suspicion. Rose was the only other person in the dorm, and she was the one who found Jack dead on the kitchen floor."

"She told me she fell asleep and didn't know anything had happened until she discovered Jack's body this morning. I've known Rose a long time, and I'm absolutely certain she is not a murderer," Chloe said with conviction.

Chloe knew that Rose was surely not a murderer, but she may have an inclination about someone else who was.

"One step at a time, Chloe. A thorough investigation has to be done before Jack's death can be officially ruled an accident. We simply have to look closely and make sure there was no one who wanted to cause him harm."

"I texted Rose when we left Dr. Block's office and let her know I'd be over in the morning. I'll make sure to gather more information then – "

"Chloe," Brian interjected firmly, "You'll do no such thing. I'm the detective. You're the dolphin trainer. And for Rose, just be her friend. Offer grief support and help with the funeral arrangements. Nothing more. Am I making myself clear?"

"Yes, Detective White. You know, you sound more like my father than my husband. I'm a big girl, and I don't need a father to tell me what I can and can't do."

"Chloe, this is no joking matter. You are pregnant with our twins. This is no time for you to be endangering your health playing investigator."

"Point taken," Chloe responded, only to calm down her husband.

She could still collect material while she and Rose were together. In order to keep her husband happy, though, she just wouldn't categorize it as investigating.

It seemed unnecessary to let Brian know her concerns about Rose at this juncture. Some private time with Rose the next day would give her more of a chance to sort out the vibes she was picking up on, without bringing Brian's judgment into play. It would also allow Rose to bring forth of her own accord any pertinent information. Chloe felt she owed her that chance out of respect for their friendship.

"Let's get these dishes cleaned up and watch a movie," Brian offered, obviously in an attempt to change the subject.

"Great idea! I'll give Gabe a teeny bit of the white rice and chicken before you take my plate."

Somehow knowing a treat was coming, Gabe moved over to his bowl and waited expectantly.

"One more thing, Brian. How long do you think it will take to clear the dorm for guests? There is a Dolphin Learners Group scheduled to start next Friday."

"Chloe, you know these things take time. Even though it will be a disappointment, that group will need to be rescheduled. There is zero chance this matter will be wrapped up by then. I'd be surprised if Theresa hasn't taken care of it already. In addition, Rose will be in no shape to cook for and host a group in just over a week. Quite frankly, I don't know how she is going to run the dorm herself. Seems like you and Theresa will have to hire her an assistant."

"I'm sure you are right. When it came to the responsibilities at the dorm, Jack was Superman. He is going to be dearly missed. No one could fill his shoes. I'm just heartbroken over his death. How will Rose move forward? I can't even imagine my life without you."

"That's enough, Dolphin Girl. I'm not going anywhere. We need to get you in front of a funny movie. Enough stress for one day."

"Yes, funny would be helpful. I need to laugh. Let's watch an 80's classic. How about *Caddy Shack?* That will distract me!"

"Good choice. I'll cue it up while you and Gabe get comfy under a quilt on the couch. No more serious talk for tonight. Okay? Tomorrow is a new day."

Let's hope it's one that brings more answers than questions when you get the autopsy report, Chloe thought to herself.

"Until tomorrow!" Chloe said as she grabbed a bottle of water and a chocolate bar to bring with her to the couch.

In her head, she was already making a list of the questions she wanted to get answers to while conducting her private investigation of Jack's death.

As long as she kept it to herself, Brian would be none the wiser.

Chapter 11

After a brief walk with an eager Gabe, Chloe and Brian set out early together for a bagel and juice.

Ann and Greg were ecstatic to see them and delivered breakfast right to their table.

"We're sorry we won't be dog-sitting your little angel for the week, but we're very happy you've decided to stay home. We were worried about you being so far away this close to your due date, Chloe," Ann said.

"Very relieved you stayed home!" Greg added. "I don't think I could have kept Ann calm for a whole week. She put on a stoic front in front of customers yesterday, but she was a wreck the rest of the day. She finally calmed down last night when you came to retrieve Gabe, and we learned the trip was cancelled."

"It's true. My stomach was in knots. My insides were twisting and turning all day. My concern was over Chloe and the babies, for sure, but once I heard about Jack's untimely death, I realized it may have been a sixth sense about him as well. I wondered if my uneasy feeling had actually been connected to his death."

"Our wives the psychics," Brian joked to Greg.

"Stop, Brian. The feelings Ann and I received are real. We are all connected through an energy field, and when something is awry with someone close to us, we can often sense it," Chloe said, really rather tired of defending her abilities, even though she knew Brian wasn't trying to hurt her feelings.

She smiled on the outside, though deep inside she knew it was this type of misunderstanding, even from her amazing husband, that kept her from mentioning the guilty aura she felt around Rose yesterday.

She trusted her senses in a way that allowed her to be less reliant on physical proof than others, but she also knew that made her vulnerable to mockery from those who didn't believe.

"If you say so, Dolphin Girl. It's just hard for me to understand because my job keeps me focused on the facts. I can't solve a case on gut feelings," Brian replied.

"I'm not so sure about that," Chloe responded. "In fact, I've got a couple of gut feelings about Jack's accident that just might prove his death wasn't an accident, after all."

Though Chloe fiercely believed in the words she had just blurted out, she knew she'd said too much.

"Chloe, we agreed last night you would not get into the investigative side of Jack's death. You promised me. And besides, you stated you were absolutely certain Rose had nothing to do with Jack's death."

"My exact words were, 'I'm absolutely certain she is not a *murderer*.' I never said I didn't think she had some idea of who may have harmed Jack. It's not that she has blood on her hands, but, when I spent time consoling her, she did seem to have a guilty conscience, and I just can't let that go. If it's something personal, she'll never talk to you about it, Brian. Rose is a deeply private, professional woman. I'm the one to talk to her. We're close friends, and that's what we do...talk. You can't deprive me of that," Chloe innocently informed her frustrated husband, judging by the smirk on his face.

"Chloe, you promised."

"Brian, we've known Chloe a lot longer than you," Greg chimed in. "And she's not going to change. If she believes

God has put her in a certain time and place for a reason, then there is no changing her mind. You might as well let it go."

Ann nodded emphatically in agreement with her husband.

"Okay. I give up," Brian said and shook his head. "You all have known Chloe since she arrived in Florida and witnessed her involvement in other cases, and you've been happily married a lot longer than us, so I'm going to reluctantly take your advice and let this go."

"Good decision," Chloe added and smiled slyly at her husband and good friends. "Being that this is the first case I've looked into while pregnant, though, I promise I'll be safer than ever and take more precautions."

"That doesn't make me feel much better," Brian said dryly.

"If I hadn't shown up in the nick of time when you were casually looking into Molly's murder, Shannon may have blown your head off."

"Something like that is not going to happen again, Brian. Chloe is over the moon to have these babies arrive. She wouldn't do anything to put their lives in jeopardy. Would you, Chloe?" Ann asked, speaking with a tone as if she were Chloe's mother encouraging a certain behavior instead of just a concerned friend.

"You have my word. All of you," Chloe stated with finality.

"Now, it's getting late, and we've got to get over to the dorm. Plus, there's a growing line, and your new employee at the counter looks completely overwhelmed."

"Mercy me!" Ann exclaimed as she turned and saw the lengthy line of customers and the panicked face of her young assistant. "Let's get this situation turned around, Greg. Chloe, please let us know if Rose needs any catering help for the funeral. We've already discussed it, and we'd like to volunteer our time, food and services."

"That's a very generous offer. I'll make sure to discuss it with Rose this morning."

"That is very kind of both of you," Brian added. "I'm sure Rose will greatly appreciate the support. Now, if I can get my wife to say goodbye, we'll be on our way."

"Very funny, Detective White. Our chat has come to a wrap! Let's get over to the dorm so I can gab with Rose."

Brian made his way to the door to hold it open for her, and Greg rushed over to help out behind the counter.

Ann leaned in to give Chloe a farewell hug, and quietly whispered in her ear, "Good job getting in the last word!"

"Ann was just giving me some advice," Chloe said, noticing the skeptical look on Brian's face as she walked through the door.

She knew he was wondering, so she thought it would be best to just put it out there. It really wasn't a lie. Ann was indeed relaying words of wisdom from her years of experience as a wife and mother.

"Okay, we'll leave it at that," Brian said, giving Chloe a funny look. "Please take it easy today. I'm sure we'll cross paths at the dorm, but when we're not together, just be careful. And what do you say we go out for some Italian tonight, so we don't have to cook?"

"Sounds terrific! And I'll be extra careful just for you, Detective White," Chloe affectionately teased as she gave him a tender hug and kiss goodbye.

Chapter 12

It was a short drive over to the dorm, but not so short that Chloe couldn't listen to a couple songs on the radio. When "Rainbow Connection," one of her favorite songs from *The Muppet Movie* came on, she was super excited.

"*We know that it's probably magic*" Chloe sang along, knowing the words backwards and forwards.

I do believe in magic, she thought to herself. And surely Rose could use a little magic right about now. Chloe couldn't even imagine how her friend was going to cope with the sudden loss of her husband. It had to be truly one of the most tragic losses a person could endure.

Once Chloe finished listening to the song, she more awkwardly than ever removed herself from the car. She slowly made her way up to the door, and as she did so, she heard a faint warbling sound.

She listened carefully and followed the noise until she came upon a small, collared dove. Chloe knew the particular type of bird because she and Brian had a pair nesting in their yard. Always eager to learn more, Chloe had taken a picture of them from a safe distance and done some research. She learned that they were not native to Florida, but rather were of a Euro-Asian background and had dispersed to the United States from the Bahamas. She also found out they mated for life.

The dove on the ground seemed on the smaller side and was still somewhat fuzzy. Its collar was still faint, and it had brown irises, rather than red, which meant it was young. It must have recently ventured out on its own.

"Hey, little guy," Chloe greeted the frightened dove. "Are you okay?"

She noticed he was holding one of his wings differently than the other. "Looks like maybe you've injured one of your wings."

Knowing in her condition she couldn't get down on the ground to help the beautiful creature, she went and rang the front doorbell to fetch someone.

"Rose, just the person I was hoping to see answer the door. I've got a situation over here, and you are the perfect person to help me."

Chloe guided Rose down the brick pathway and stopped beside one of the hibiscus bushes. "This fuzzy guy seems like he could use our help. His right wing is somewhat askance. What do you think?"

"He's definitely in trouble. Otherwise, he'd have flown off by now. Why don't I grab a box, line it with a towel and scoop him up? We'll need to take him over to Dr. Shelley right away. You stay here with him, and I'll be right back."

"Sounds like a plan. But, I'm not supposed to be out in the sun for too long."

"No worries. Why don't I stay outside then, and you grab the items from the kitchen? You know where the towels are, and there are a couple of boxes in the recycling bin from the party. Please let Brian know we'll have to delay my interview. We won't be long, though I know he'll be upset."

"First things first," Chloe spoke up. "Brian will understand that."

"If you say so," Rose muttered under her breath.

"You just focus on your well-being right now, Rose, and I'll take care of Brian."

"Thanks, Chloe. You're just the person I need with me right now. I'm just sorry you missed your trip."

"I'm right where I'm supposed to be," Chloe assured her friend.

And with that, she headed inside, while Rose cautiously sat down next to the dove to keep it calm.

Chapter 13

As she entered the front hall of the dorm, Chloe called out to Brian. When he immediately popped out from around the corner, he surprised her.

"What's up, Dolphin Girl? Are you looking for Rose? She was here just a few minutes ago."

"Nice job firing off questions, Detective White! Did you mistake the front hall for an interrogation room and me for your suspect?" Chloe responded with feigned snark.

"Very funny. With the aid of those pregnancy hormones, you are a regular comedian!"

"Ha, ha," Chloe replied. "But to answer your questions in order…I've come inside to grab a towel and a box and to let you know that I found an injured dove on my way up the path a few minutes ago, and it needs to go to the vet. Rose is sitting with it while she waits for me to get the supplies. She'll have to speak with you this afternoon."

"Chloe, where did you find a dove? Only a few minutes before you, I walked up the same pathway and I didn't notice anything out of the ordinary."

"That's because you were probably rushing, Detective White. I, on the other hand, was safely taking my time, and as always, listening to the sounds of nature around me."

"And you're much more in tune with your natural surroundings now that you're required to slow down for our babies, so point taken…"

"And I sort of like it. It really is nice to stop and smell the roses. And in this case, listen and hear an animal in need."

"Very true. Let me help you retrieve the things from the kitchen. Please let Rose know I'll interview her this afternoon. Right now, it's most important to save this bird's life. Besides, there's nothing more any of us can do for Jack, he's gone forever."

"Maybe just bring him justice," Chloe said, a little surprised that Brian was taking this interruption of his investigation so well.

"That remains to be seen. From what I can tell so far, his death continues to look like an accident."

Chapter 14

With supplies in hand, Chloe made her way out to Rose who was still sitting on the ground speaking softly to the sweet dove.

"Here's everything," she said as she handed the items to Rose. "Why don't you carefully put him in on the towel? I'll drive, and you can hold the box. I don't think it would fit on my big belly."

"Sounds like a plan. Did you run into Brian? Does he know I'm heading with you over to the vet's office?"

"He does, and he was pretty cool about it. He'll talk to you this afternoon."

"Thanks for handling that matter."

"No worries. You have enough to manage. I'll handle Brian."

"Thanks, Chloe. I truly appreciate that. Now let's get this little guy over to Dr. Shelley. She'll know what to do with him."

"That's true – she's the best."

As they drove over to their vet's office, Chloe and Rose chatted comfortably. They knew Dr. Shelley very well. She had taken care of all the dolphins at Dolphin Connection since the facility opened. She was truly an angel on Earth.

The further they traveled from the dorm, Chloe couldn't help but notice that Rose's rigid shoulders softened and her tense voice relaxed. She wondered if the diversion of the small injured bird was the reason, or if her friend had less of a guilty conscience now that a larger distance separated her from the scene of the accident.

"Here we are," Chloe said, pulling her Mustang into the small parking lot.

Since it was just mid-morning, the place wasn't too crowded yet. Chloe struggled to get herself out of the car and then around to open the door for Rose.

"Why don't you hold the box, Chloe, while I slip out of the car and then I'll take it from you to carry inside?"

"Sounds like a plan," Chloe said.

The two women maneuvered their way out of the car and through the door of Dr. Shelley's.

"Hi, Ladies! Is this the little dove you found? Dr. Shelley said you should bring him right back."

"How did you know we were coming, Patrice?" Chloe asked the helpful assistant who had worked for Dr. Shelley the last few years.

"Your husband called to let us know you were on the way. He's worried about both of you. I'm so sorry for your loss, Rose. Please accept my deepest condolences," Patrice said, leaning over to put her arm around Rose.

"Thank you so much. I'm still in a state of shock. I don't know what I'm going to do without Jack. It seems like we've been together for as long as I can remember. The dorm has been 'a home away from home' for the Dolphin Learners students because of him," Rose said, her voice shaky with emotion.

"Because of you, too," Chloe reminded her friend, "though there certainly will be a void left now that Jack is gone."

"I think finding this little guy was a Godsend," Rose said. "It helps to focus on something other than my own grief."

"I agree," Patrice replied. "I started working here soon after I lost my Dad, and the animals have greatly helped me heal. They are our angels on Earth."

"That they are," all three women said in unison as a voice came down the hallway and interrupted their conversation.

"Have Chloe and Rose arrived with the baby dove?" Dr. Shelley yelled down the hallway.

"We're here!" Chloe and Rose sang in almost perfect harmony.

After years of working around a noisy office full of a wide array of animals, Dr. Shelley always had to be the loudest voice in the place to be heard at all.

"Bring that little guy back here so I can check him out."

"We're on our way. Thanks, Patrice! We'll see you on the way out," Chloe said.

As Chloe and Rose brought the young dove into the examination room, Dr. Shelley took the box, placed it on the table and scooped out the small bird.

"I believe it's a collared dove, probably on the younger side," Chloe said.

"You're absolutely right, Chloe. He appears to be not much more than a fledgling. Probably hasn't been long since he left the nest. Actually, that may be when he injured his wing. It can be trial and error in the beginning, similar to a baby learning to walk. Most get along just fine, but some stumble and take really hard falls. Looks like that's what happened to this sweetie pie. We'll take an x-ray of his wing, so we know for sure," Dr. Shelley said as she whisked the dove off the table and left the room.

Chloe and Rose stayed put, knowing the pair would be back shortly.

"He is really calm, isn't he?" Chloe asked Rose.

"Definitely. As we know all too well, most animals are considerably shaken up when they are injured. He seemed grateful we found him."

"He has a special energy, that's for sure," Chloe said. "I don't think we found him by accident."

"I agree 100%," Rose said. "Maybe Jack sent him to us because he knew we could help him, and he would help us."

"My sentiments exactly," Chloe agreed.

"Well, looks like his right wing does have a slight fracture. It should heal quickly, though, because he is so young. And it does appear, by the way, from the x-ray that he is a male. Are one of you interested in nursing him back to health? They won't take him at a local sanctuary because collared doves aren't native to Florida."

"I'll take him," Rose quickly asserted with conviction. "He's just what I need right now."

"That's right. I'm so sorry, Rose. I got caught up with our little friend and failed to express my condolences. Jack was a good man, through and through. He will be dearly missed."

"Thank you, Dr. Shelley. He had a deep respect for you and all you've done for so many animals throughout your career. I'd like to make a donation in his name to your practice."

"That would be very thoughtful. I, too, think that would mean a lot to Jack," Dr. Shelley said.

"Do you think our baby dove will be able to return to the wild when he heals, Dr. Shelley?" Chloe asked.

"That remains to be seen and will probably be up to him. We'll have to see how well he can fly when his wing heals. Surely, his health and safety will be our top priority. For now, why don't you get him a large cage and some appropriate food and water supply. He's old enough to eat seed at this point, so you won't need to use an eye dropper. Doves are highly intelligent, so talk to him often. Those raised in human care can become highly social with their human counterparts."

"That won't be a problem," Rose assured the concerned vet. "It's going to be just the two of us in the house this week, so I'll probably be talking to him a lot. Our group that was supposed to begin next Friday has already been postponed, and I've been dreading the silence with Jack gone. It's sad to say that, at this point, the investigators have actually been decent company."

"It's going to be a hard adjustment," Chloe said as she comforted her friend with a hug, "but we're all going to help you. This sweet guy just might be the best medicine for your grief."

"That's true," Dr. Shelley agreed. "And before you leave, we need to put a name on his file. What do you want to call him?"

"Fuzzy! His name just has to be Fuzzy. I knew the moment I saw him," Rose said. "That was my nickname for Jack because he was warm and fuzzy like a teddy bear."

"Fuzzy it is," Dr. Shelley said as she noted the name in the medical file she was holding. "Rose, please let me know when you are holding a service for Jack. I definitely want to attend."

"Thank you, Dr. Shelley. I was thinking about this Sunday. That will only give us a few days to plan, but I believe we can pull it together. Theresa has already confirmed that we can hold the service at Dolphin Connection on Sunday and close the facility to visitors for the day."

"There isn't a more perfect place to celebrate Jack's life. DC was his home, and our dolphins his soul mates," Chloe said, the hairs on her arms standing at attention as a spiritually-charged energy shot through her body, a sign that their plans were definitely in alignment with what Jack would want.

"Yes, indeed," Dr. Shelley agreed. "Now let me know if you ladies need anything. I'm always here for you."

"Thanks!" Chloe and Rose both belted out.

As they looked at each other and laughed at their perfect timing, Chloe joked, "We sing so well together maybe we should form a duet!"

"Great idea," Rose said, "We could call it '2 WISH' for the two of us and all of the wishes we hope will come true in the world!"

"I like that," Chloe said and nodded.

"Maybe you two are getting ahead of yourself," Dr. Shelley interrupted. "Chloe, you're a dolphin trainer who is about to have twins, and Rose, you're a dolphin handler who feeds and houses hundreds of students at the dorm each year. I think you both have your hands full for now. That is a great name for a duet though, I'll give you that."

"You're right, Dr. Shelley. Though it was fun to dream for a moment about being an entertainer. And there's probably already a real 2 WISH out there. I love that name," Chloe said.

Chloe and Rose said their farewell to Dr. Shelley and Patrice as they left the homey office and were on their way.

They decided to head back to the dorm so that Fuzzy and Chloe could rest inside. Meanwhile, Rose would head to the pet store to purchase a cage and food. She'd also pick up lunch for she, Chloe, Brian and the other investigators.

"Are you sure you want to host lunch today?" Chloe asked.

"Right now, having other things to focus on is saving my sanity, Chloe. Otherwise, I'd be curled up in bed in the fetal position. Jack would want me to continue to function productively, and I intend to do just that."

"Very smart, my dear friend," Chloe responded. "Let's get Fuzzy set up in his new home and fill the bellies of Brian and his colleagues. That will put him in the best mood possible when he interviews you this afternoon."

"I had almost forgotten about that," Rose muttered under her breath.

"Better to get it done before the sun sets on another day," Chloe encouraged her. "Besides, you have nothing to worry about, just tell Brian what you told me."

"I wish it were that simple," Rose mumbled even more softly, almost to herself.

"What did you say?" Chloe asked, unable to hide her concern at her friend's revelation.

"Nothing," Rose said. "Really, it's nothing."

"Okay," Chloe replied. "I'm not going to push you now. But, if there is something you need to share, you know you can trust me."

"You are the one person I know I can fully trust, Chloe," Rose said with gratitude in her voice.

"I'm here when you're ready," Chloe told her nervous friend and then left it at that.

She knew there was no use pressuring Rose to talk before she was ready. The conversation had confirmed one thing, though. Chloe's suspicion that Rose had an air of guilt around her was spot on.

Chloe had no better idea of what that guilt was connected to than she had the night before, but time would tell her. Luckily, with a week of vacation in front of her, all Chloe had was time.

Chapter 15

Relaxing with Fuzzy and waiting for Rose to return, Chloe realized it would be a great time to try and reach Grace. She knew they were stopping in Charleston, South Carolina the previous night and were probably seeing a couple of local sights before they set out for Williamsburg.

She picked up her phone and dialed her twin.

Grace picked up after just a few rings.

"Hey, Sis! How are you feeling?" Grace immediately asked. "I've been thinking of you and meaning to call, but we were squeezing in some sightseeing this morning before we hit the road again."

"I'm feeling well today. Thanks for asking. I'm at the dorm now waiting for Rose to return with bird supplies and lunch."

"Did you say bird supplies? When we were at the dorm for your baby shower the other night, I didn't notice a bird."

"We just found it this morning on the front pathway. We brought it to our vet, who confirmed that his wing is injured. He'll need a safe place to recover and some tender love and care, and Rose is just the person to provide it right now."

"That definitely is true. Maybe this is the diversion she needs to help cope with her grief."

"Exactly my thought. Fuzzy, that is what we named him, is a collared dove, and he is very sweet. At the moment, he is taking a rest on top of my big belly. The babies are stirring like crazy, but it doesn't seem to bother him."

"Between the dolphins, Gabe and now Fuzzy, those twins are going to come into this world already loving animals."

"I can't even imagine that they wouldn't. They'll probably be kindred spirits," Chloe affirmed.

"It will be interesting to watch them grow and develop connections with their own favorite animals," Grace replied.

"I can't wait. It won't be long now. In the meantime, I'm enjoying the end of my pregnancy. I don't know if I'll get to do this again, and even though it sometimes gets unbearably uncomfortable, I wouldn't trade it for anything in the world," Chloe said, meaning every word with every piece of her heart.

"It is a very special experience. I agree with you. I'm glad you are feeling back to yourself today. You had us worried. We were relieved to get Brian's text that all went smoothly at your doctor. What's on your schedule after lunch today?" Grace asked.

"Rose has to meet with Brian to answer some questions, and I'm going to stay nearby to support her. After that, if she is up to it, I may try to help her hash out an outline for the funeral service. She plans to hold it this Sunday at Dolphin Connection, so we only have a few days to pull everything together," Chloe informed her sister.

"Dolphin Connection will be a beautiful place to honor Jack. With your help, I'm sure Rose will manage to successfully plan a fitting tribute."

"Thank you, Gracie. I'm trying to be a positive support system for her. She needs a solid friend right now. This morning, she indicated that there was something she wanted to get off her chest, but she wasn't ready yet, so I didn't push her," Chloe said.

"Maybe after the funeral she'll be ready to open up," Grace offered.

"Maybe," Chloe agreed. "As we always say, first things first. When Brian conducts his interview with her this afternoon, he'll get the pertinent information from the night of the accident, but I doubt she'll offer any additional background, if she doesn't need to. Whatever it is that she's holding close, it seems very personal in nature."

"Be patient, Chloe. Just be her friend. Let Brian do the investigative work," Grace reminded her.

"Okay, but sometimes he needs my help," Chloe reminded her well-meaning sister.

"I think he was a successful detective long before he met you, sweetie," Grace said.

"True, but he's even better with my help!"

"What was that you said?" Brian asked.

Chloe had no idea Brian was anywhere near her or she would not have blurted that out.

"Uh, nothing. Nothing, at all," she quickly, probably too quickly, responded. "I'm just wrapping up with Grace."

"Okay, if you say so, Dolphin Girl. Since you're pregnant with our twins, I'm giving you a lot of extra understanding. Don't expect this to last once the babies are born," Brian joked.

With a sideways glance, Chloe let her husband know she was done with his humor for the moment.

"Lunch should be here soon. Let me finish up with Gracie first."

"Go ahead, sweetie. Send Grace, Matt and the kids my love."

"Doing it right now. I'll see you in a few minutes," Chloe assured him.

"Sorry about that, Grace. Brian walked in at just the wrong moment."

"He caught you talking about him, huh?" Grace said and laughed.

"Maybe," Chloe admitted. "On a more positive note, he sends his love to you all."

"Right back at him. And please, Chloe, give the man a break. He doesn't want you to get involved in a case while you're this far along in your pregnancy," Grace said.

"He doesn't want me getting involved in his cases, pregnant or not. But, that's tough. If I think I can help, I can't keep my nose out of something. Sometimes, my senses are very in-tune with my surroundings and lead me towards clues others might not uncover. It doesn't seem right to ignore a special gift God has given me. If I can help, I have to help. Period," Chloe explained to her twin.

"Of all people, I get it, Chloe. You've had an extra sensitive sixth sense since we were children. It is your calling to use it to help others, and I'm behind you 100%. But things are changing. You are going to be a mother soon, and that means, you have to make the choice to be more careful. You don't have to become a nervous Nellie, just try to find a better balance, that's all. If you can exhibit a bit more self-control when it comes to your inclination to figure out mysteries, I'm sure Brian will be extremely relieved."

"Advice taken, Grace. And only because it's coming from you. I trust your judgment implicitly and will keep it in mind, I promise. Now moving on, what adventure did you go on this morning in Charleston?" Chloe asked, in an attempt to change the subject.

"We took a boat ride out to Fort Sumter and spent a couple hours exploring the island. And we're about to sit down for a delicious seafood lunch at our hotel which overlooks a Navy ship and submarine. Then, if we want to reach Williamsburg before it gets too late in the evening, we need to get on the road."

"I'm going to let you go. Please send me some pictures and details from Fort Sumter when you get a chance," Chloe requested.

"I'll do that when we're in the car and Matt's taking his turn driving."

"Perfect. I'll enjoy looking at them when I snuggle up with Gabe on the couch tonight. Enjoy your lunch and safe travels to Virginia."

"Thanks! And you have a delicious lunch, too, when Rose arrives!"

"Actually, I think I hear her coming in now. I'm going to put Fuzzy in his box and go help her."

"Did he rest on your tummy the whole time we talked?" Grace asked.

"Indeed, he did! And quite contentedly. He seems to be at ease with people, which is a good thing, since he'll be living at the dorm while he recovers, and it's often a busy place."

"Sounds like he'll be right at home," Grace replied.

Chloe heard Rose call for her.

"Tell the kids I miss them," Chloe said and bid her twin a final farewell.

"They miss you tons," Grace replied. "You are definitely the fun Aunt. I'll have my work cut out for me to reach such a grand level when your twins are born."

"You'll be the best," Chloe reassured her.

"Thanks. Until we talk again - love you more than anything in the world," Grace said.

"And I, you," Chloe returned, as she ended the call.

She gently placed Fuzzy in his box and carefully walked to the kitchen to join Rose and the others.

Chapter 16

Lunch was delicious...and boisterous.

In addition to Brian and his partner, there were two crime scene investigators at the dorm, which made for a full table.

Once they had all shared the spread of seafood choices Rose had brought home, including salmon for Chloe, they all wanted to hear how things had gone at the vet's office.

There was something special about sunny Florida, Chloe thought to herself, that brought about an affinity for animals amongst many of the residents, regardless of their professions. It no longer amazed her when she saw a police officer stop to help a turtle cross the road.

Chloe let Rose inform everyone about Fuzzy. She thought it a productive distraction for her grieving friend. It would also keep her mind occupied before she had to sit down and talk with Brian.

Chloe was eager to hear if Rose would share any pertinent information with Brian that could help determine if Jack's death had been an accident. And she was also curious as to whether or not Brian had discovered any leads in that direction.

She and Rose had been so caught up with Fuzzy and then lunch, there really hadn't been anytime for them to privately discuss the matter. Maybe that was for the best, Chloe thought to herself. Maybe, this time, she really would leave the investigating to Brian. That would truly be a miracle for which Brian would be undoubtedly grateful.

"Are you all done?" Brian asked as he attempted to clear Chloe's plate.

He'd startled her, so her reply was a bit delayed. "Um, yes, I'm all set. Thank you," she managed to get out, stumbling over her words.

"Are you okay, Chloe? Have you drank enough fluids today?" Brian asked.

"I'm fine, I'm fine," she said, always grateful for his sweet concern over her wellbeing. "I've been inside most of the day, and I've had more than enough water. I was just thinking about something, that's all."

"You're not having any Braxton Hicks today are you?" Brian continued his interrogation.

"No, I'm not, Dr. White!" Chloe retorted. "What was that you were saying recently about letting each of us do our respective jobs? Somehow, I don't think Dr. Block needs any help. He's got the pregnancy thing covered."

"Yes, I'm sure he does, Dolphin Girl, and I'm glad to hear you're so intent on people sticking to their own jobs. That is the way it should be," Brian said, a victorious smile on his face.

"I walked right into that, didn't I," Chloe acquiesced.

"Yes, you did. And it's nice for me to have the last word, once in awhile," Brian replied.

"Very true. For now, why don't we leave it at that? I'm going to head over to Dolphin Connection to say a quick hello to my human and marine friends, while you and Rose converse."

"Just take it easy and stay out of the sun. You're supposed to be on vacation, remember?" Brian reminded her.

"Don't push it, Detective, not Doctor. Remember that," Chloe shot back at him.

"Didn't take long for you to get the last word again, Dolphin Girl!" Brian joked.

"Love you, sweetheart. That's all I have to say," she replied.

"Love you, too, Dolphin Girl. That's why I worry," Brian reminded her.

"I know. You have a big heart, and I love that about you," Chloe said, as if he didn't know.

"I'll see you both later this afternoon then," she said to him and Rose as she got up to leave.

"Why don't we get Fuzzy set up in his cage before you leave," Rose suggested.

"Absolutely, I almost forgot!" Chloe admitted. "I got so caught up in my thoughts. Let's do it – Brian, could you help us assemble the cage before you and Rose talk?"

"I'm happy to help," Brian offered.

They all knew this was something Jack would have tended to if he were here, but no one said it.

"Come on, lovely ladies, let's get Fuzzy comfortable in his new digs," Brian beckoned.

"Coming!" Rose and Chloe piped up together, each grateful for the productive distraction and for the capable man at their service.

Chapter 17

Once they had Fuzzy set up in his new home, a very large and beautiful bird cage, Chloe left Rose to sit down with Brian. Rather than drive, she decided to slowly walk over to the grounds of Dolphin Connection, in order to get some low-impact exercise.

She decided to drop by and see Theresa first. Alternating her time outside and inside would keep her cool. She peeked her head around the corner of Theresa's office and saw that her friend and colleague was indeed inside.

"Hi there! Do you have a moment to talk?" Chloe asked a surprised Theresa.

"Chloe, of course! I wasn't expecting to see you here. You know you're supposed to be on vacation, right?"

"Yes, and you know I consider being here a vacation even when I'm working," Chloe offered with heartfelt conviction.

"I couldn't agree more myself. And I'm so glad you stopped by. I've been meaning to give you a call, but things have been busy, and I knew you were with your family yesterday," Theresa explained.

"I was, and they're off to Virginia now. This morning, I've been with Rose. I went to the dorm this morning to comfort her, and we ended up rescuing a young collared dove that was out on the front pathway."

"Did you take him over to Dr. Shelley?" Theresa asked, concern filling her voice.

"Absolutely. She did an x-ray which showed a fractured wing, so she recommended Rose nursing him back to health for the time being. Once we see how he heals, Dr. Shelley will decide if he can be returned to the wild," Chloe said.

"Helping an injured bird sounds like something positive to keep Rose's mind off Jack's tragic death. Maybe helping the dove will keep her from becoming overwhelmed with grief," Theresa expressed.

"Exactly, a diversion sent from above," Chloe agreed. "Rose needs to be able to think somewhat straight in the next few days while she plans Jack's service, and then her emotions can pour out. By the way, she mentioned you offered for her to hold the service Sunday here on the grounds."

"Yes, I hope you're in agreement. It seemed like the best way to support Rose and to make the service accessible for a large group of people. I've already placed an order to rent folding chairs that we can set up by the underwater viewing area. The more formal part of the service can be held there and then everyone can walk along the docks, if Rose would like to have all the dolphins do something special," Theresa said.

"Perfect on both points," Chloe said and nodded. "Thank you for renting the chairs. Let's coordinate the dolphins together. Hopefully, Rose will be able to select the prayers and passages from the Bible she'd like to include."

"It will be difficult for her to focus on all this right now, but very important so that the service is a true reflection of Jack's spirit," Theresa said.

"I agree. Together, we'll bolster Rose and honor Jack. Anything else new you'd like to share before I go visit a few beautiful faces?" Chloe asked.

"Actually, my day began with some great news that I've been wanting to relay to you first," a giddy Theresa said.

"Please share – your excitement has me very curious," Chloe informed her friend.

"Well, we've made it to the top of the list. On Saturday morning, we'll be receiving a male dolphin named Nix who will be visiting with us for six months. He'll bring a whole new DNA profile to our Dolphin Connection pod, and hopefully, at least one of our mature females will be pregnant before he leaves," Theresa said, beaming with joy.

"That is amazing news! I can't wait to meet him! I'll make sure to be here Saturday morning when he arrives to help ease his transition into our facility," Chloe said, wanting to cheer.

"Thanks, Chloe. I knew you'd be as thrilled as I am!"

"Where is he coming from?" Chloe asked.

"He was originally rescued in New Orleans during Hurricane Katrina, along with several other bottlenose. He has spent time visiting a couple of other facilities since then and is very easily adaptable. If things go well, we can apply for him to make Dolphin Connection his permanent home. Now that would be wonderful, wouldn't it?"

Chloe was ecstatic. "I couldn't think of a better gift. God is truly shining down on us as we have to say goodbye to our dear friend Jack. A new member of our family can't replace one of the old, but it will surely help the healing process. God is sending us an angel," Chloe acknowledged, full of gratitude.

"Each of our dolphins has been heaven sent – each individual a precious gift. Nix couldn't be arriving at a better time," Theresa affirmed.

"Just like finding Fuzzy this morning. All things happen in God's perfect timing," Chloe said. "And now is the perfect time for me to visit with my favorite girls, human and dolphin," Chloe said.

"Please keep the news of Nix's arrival and subsequent stay quiet until I send out an official letter this afternoon," Theresa mentioned.

"No worries! I'll just whisper it to the dolphins, though with their intuition, they probably already know he's on the way," Chloe shared.

"I'm sure they do, and they'll keep it to themselves, so we don't have to worry about them," Theresa joked.

"If they could speak English...we'd all be in trouble. They've heard all our life stories," Chloe said and chuckled.

"Very true," Theresa said and laughed softly in agreement. "They'd have many, many stories to tell."

"I think we're safe for now! If we arrive one morning, and the dolphins have learned to hold a journal in one flipper and a pen in the other, then we'll worry," Chloe responded, her heart filled with light and admiration for her highly-adept dolphin friends.

Theresa smiled and stood up and came around the desk to give Chloe a warm hug.

"Go spend some time with your girls and be careful not to get overheated today," Theresa said.

"Dr. White has already covered that today, and, in case you're wondering, too, I'm drinking plenty of water," Chloe assured her always-concerned mentor as she held up her water canteen. "I'm being extra cautious. Yesterday was scary for me, too."

"We only worry because we love you," Theresa said with a wink.

"And I appreciate that," Chloe confessed. "I'm going to head down to the docks and then see if I can make plans to meet up with Bailey, Jenna and Eliza for dessert this evening."

"Keep me posted on the plans for the service, and I'll make sure to update you with any pertinent news concerning Nix's arrival," Theresa relayed.

"Sounds good. Enjoy your afternoon, sister friend."

"You too, Chloe. Be careful on the floating docks!"

Chloe shook her head and laughed as she waved and exited Theresa's office.

She knew her family and friends only worried because they loved her, but, lately, it was over the top. Chloe could get up and down from all the floating docks blindfolded, if necessary. She had spent so much time in and around the dolphin's home, she could virtually feel her way around it.

She was pregnant, for goodness sake, not incapacitated!

She carefully, for the sake of the worriers, made her way around the dock to visit with all the dolphins and then went straight to her office to cool off and drink some water.

Somehow sensing the heaviness in her soul, the dolphins had been rather silly. In an attempt to wash away the tears that ran down her face, they splashed, squeaked and dove. All at once, her grief from Jack's death had risen up inside of her, and some of it leaked out.

She had been very close with Jack. He had often leant her a comforting ear and offered her kind words of support. They were kindred spirits, sharing a deep love for the animals that surrounded them and the desire to educate people about them.

Chloe had been so busy trying to make sure Rose was surviving, she forgot how much she was going to miss her friend. The dolphins, as always, provided a safe place to let her emotions flow.

By the time she made it back to her office, she had shed many tears. She rested, drank, wiped her eyes and pulled herself together.

After a few minutes, she set out to find her friends and make plans to get together. Fortunately, the other ladies enjoyed dessert as much as she did, and so she didn't have to convince any of them that sitting down for treats together would help them organize ideas for Jack's service.

Chloe's favorite spot was still Sprinkles, and she had made loyal customers of most of her friends as well. So, they settled on meeting up there later that evening.

When Chloe returned to the dorm, Rose and Brian had already finished up.

Rounding the corner before the conference room, she found her grieving friend crying on the floor. She was also telling someone to stop calling her and contacting her online. She sounded distraught and was in the process of throwing her phone on the floor when she noticed Chloe, and it startled her.

"Rose, what's going on?! Are you okay?!" Chloe asked, so concerned she didn't really know what to do.

"I'm fine, I'm fine," Rose replied, grabbing her phone and quickly pushing herself up from the floor. "It's nothing really, just an old friend that keeps contacting me. He's making me uncomfortable, that's all. I can handle it. Nothing you need to worry about, Chloe."

"I'm very worried, Rose. Nobody should be giving you a hard time...now or ever. Does this gentleman know you just lost your husband?" Chloe questioned.

"I'm not sure. I didn't have a conversation with him. All I did was tell him to stop contacting me," Rose replied. "He's just lonely and wants someone to talk to, but I'm not the person for that job, and he needs to leave me alone."

"Did you tell Brian about this person, Rose? Could he possibly have something to do with Jack's death?"

"Absolutely not…on both fronts!" Rose firmly replied, almost shouting. "Brian doesn't need to know about my personal business, and there is no way possible this person has anything to do with Jack's death!"

"You can't know that for sure," Chloe said, confused and startled by such strange behavior from her close friend, "and I believe the reason Brian met with you today was to learn about your personal business. That's what detectives do, they find out what is happening in someone's personal life, so they can figure out whether or not a crime has occurred and who committed it. You absolutely cannot hold back pertinent information from Brian, Rose. If he finds out you weren't truthful with him, he'll be furious. Honesty is a really big deal to him. Please reconsider," Chloe pleaded.

"There's nothing more to share with him. Please drop it, Chloe. You're my friend, and you promised to be here for me, and I'm asking you to drop it. Trust that I know what I'm doing," Rose begged her.

Feeling great empathy for her friend's difficult situation, Chloe agreed to stay quiet, though she wasn't happy about it.

"I'll keep this to myself, for now, Rose, because I can't stand to see you in so much distress. Your grief over Jack's death is more than enough for you to handle, at this time. Trust is key in a friendship, and I trust you implicitly. I know you would discuss this matter with Brian if you felt it had any connection to what happened here Tuesday night."

"Chloe, you can trust me. And from our discussion, it appeared as if Brian actually may have a couple of leads. He can fill you in on those later."

"So, he's not sure Jack's fall was an accident? Quite frankly, it doesn't feel like an accident to me either, Rose. Jack was too aware of his surroundings to slip and fall on an ice pick. My gut is telling me someone intentionally harmed your husband, and I, for one, am not going to rest until we figure out who that person is," Chloe stated, letting Rose know she wasn't backing down just because she'd decided not to say anything for now.

"Chloe, please…let it go. Just be my friend. Brian can handle the detective work. It's not healthy for you to be getting caught up in all this stress at this point in your pregnancy," Rose said, sounding more and more desperate to keep Chloe out of the investigation.

"I'll keep my mouth closed for now," Chloe assured her worried friend, "but I'm not making any long-term promises. Ultimately, your safety is tantamount. If someone hurt Jack, that person could harm you, too."

"Nobody hurt Jack, Chloe. He slipped and fell on that ice pick. It was a horrible accident. He was tired and must have lost his balance. Please leave it at that. Now, let's check on our furry friend," Rose suggested, walking out of the room, evidently hoping Chloe would forget their heated conversation and follow her to check Fuzzy.

Chloe was stunned by her friend's behavior, but tried to recover quickly, so Rose didn't realize just how blown away and filled with suspicion she now was.

"I'm right behind you," Chloe called out.

The only thing that would keep Chloe from revealing to Brian the events that had just taken place was her overwhelming empathy for Rose. She could only imagine that losing your life partner had to be unbearable, rocking one's world to the core. Nothing short of such a deep loss could have ever convinced her to briefly abandon her own code of ethics.

Just for the moment, she'd let her shock and concern over her friend's outburst take a front seat to her own moral convictions. But even as she made her decision, Chloe was afraid she'd regret it.

She knew her friend was trying to change the direction of their interaction, and she went along with it. She'd gather more information from Brian at dinner. The autopsy results should be in, too.

"Just promise me you'll open up when you're ready," Chloe asked Rose as they held Fuzzy between them.

"I promise," Rose agreed.

"Thank you," Chloe responded. "I am going to meet with the girls for dessert to coordinate a few parts of the service. Do you want to meet me for bagels in the morning so we can review everything, including a program? The sooner we have that set, the easier it will be for me to get it printed. I have many pictures of Dolphin Learner students with Jack from over the years, and I'll plan to put together a slide show, if that's okay with you."

"That would be wonderful. And I'd love for you to officiate the service, as well, from the greeting to the farewell. You've been a true friend to me Chloe, and I appreciate that. I believe it was Thomas Aquinas who said, 'There is nothing on this earth more to be prized than true friendship.'"

"Truer words couldn't be spoken," Chloe agreed. "Rose, I know you would do the same for me. Now please try to get some rest tonight. Hopefully, Fuzzy will help keep you company. Maybe try reading to him. I saw an article somewhere that showed animals find stories soothing."

"I'll try it out and let you know. Do you want to meet at nine in the morning at Ann and Greg's store?"

"Sounds good. That will give me some extra time to sleep in. Since I'm technically on vacation, I should make the most of it," Chloe joked.

"You better savor it before those babies are born," Rose said.

"Very true. I'm tired just thinking about it. Now let me give you a hug and find Brian to say goodbye."

Chloe gave her newly widowed colleague a long, supportive hug and then bid Fuzzy and her husband farewell before she took off. Out of the corner of her eye, she caught Rose watching her embrace Brian, and guilt crept into her conscience that her own husband was alive and well. She knew that feeling contributed to her temporary, though erratic, decision to honor Rose's request for silence.

She couldn't wait to meet Brian for Italian food that evening. They had a lot to talk about, for sure.

But first, she'd head home to spend some quality time with her favorite furry friend, Gabriel. She could almost sense him getting antsy and wanted to reassure him as soon as possible that he was still "top dog' in her life. How he would handle things when two new babies arrived was anyone's guess. Chloe believed their relationship would be purely magical!

Chapter 18

Dinner at Ciao was excellent, as always. Chloe and Brian had been going there since their first date. Laura, their waitress, knew them well, and the moment they walked through the door, placed their standing order.

Since the pregnancy, the only thing that had changed was Chloe's drink order. She now had Pellegrino sparkling water to drink in place of a glass of white wine. It was both refreshing and bubbly, an explosion of hydration.

Chloe ate Italian food so often, she was convinced the twins would be born already having a taste for it!

Before they caught up on the news of the day, she and Brian made a point of enjoying their meals.

Being that Brian already knew about her day, at least as much as she wanted him to know at this point, she let him go ahead and fill her in on what he had learned about Jack's death.

Her eagerness to hear about the autopsy had to be palpable, but Brian seemed reluctant to share the news he had learned with her.

"Just tell me," Chloe pleaded. "What's your hesitation? I'm going to learn the truth, inevitably. And I'd prefer it to be sooner, rather than later, so I'll know what type of support Rose is going to need. Understandably, her emotions will be different if Jack's death was a murder as opposed to an accident."

"Very true, and without a doubt, you will find out the facts whether it's from me or from another source.

Personally, I'd prefer the latter. The longer I can protect you from any possible harm, the better," Brian said, fiddling with his napkin.

"Sweetheart, you can't keep me shielded from the real world. I'm a big girl and surely you believe that I can take care of myself," Chloe said, even though she loved his fierce desire to keep her and their babies safe.

"That is a given. You were taking care of yourself long before we met, but it is different now. You are my other half, and I couldn't bear for anything to happen to you. And your health is fragile right now. You are in your final trimester of a high-risk pregnancy. There's no room for you to take any chances, Chloe. Before I share the autopsy findings, do you promise we are on the same page?" Brian asked, begging her with his eyes to do as he wished.

"I promise. You know how I feel about these babies. I'm not going to do anything that would jeopardize their lives. I'm carrying them, and it's my responsibility to protect them from harm," Chloe said, trying to ease her concerned husband. "Trust me, just trust me."

"I do, and I'm sure you've guessed by now that Jack was murdered. This afternoon, the Coroner officially declared it to be a homicide on the death certificate. Evidently, the angle of the wound made it impossible to have been an accident. Someone shorter than Jack stabbed him at an upward angle, and then it appears that, Jack fell face forward with the ice pick in his chest. If he'd slipped and fell on it in some freak accident, it would have been impossible for it to have entered him that way."

"I knew it," Chloe declared. "I sensed it right away. This was no accident. But, who on Earth would want to murder Jack?! The man had no enemies. He was truly one of the sweetest, kindest, gentlest souls I've ever met. When you spoke to Rose this afternoon, were you able to uncover any leads?"

"Nothing definitive," Brian responded, "but I had a feeling she wasn't being completely forthright with me."

"How so?" Chloe asked, hoping he was just as suspicious as she was so she wouldn't feel as guilty about not quite telling him everything.

"It's hard to put my finger on it, but it just felt like she was leaving something out. Even the smallest tidbit of information can help us figure out a case, and I'm not sure Rose fully comprehends that point, though I passionately tried to explain it to her."

"We can all be a little stubborn when we don't want to hear the truth," Chloe responded, trying to cover up Brian's concerns, and her own, with a bit of humor.

"Wise words coming from a woman who possesses fierce determination herself when she sets her mind on an idea," Brian said with a smirk.

"Thank you for the compliment, though I'm not sure it was meant to be taken in such a positive light."

"It was in a way," Brian responded. "Your stubbornness can both impress me and infuriate me, depending on the situation and whether or not you are keeping your personal safety your top priority."

"Safety first, Mr. White, always safety first. Just like all the branding says on the baby products," Chloe said, rather proud of her clever comeback.

"Well, if it's right for babies, then it's right for their parents," Brian said, turning the joke back on Chloe. "We should make a big sign that hangs in the kitchen to remind you of that, Dolphin Girl. You are the epitome of a loving, cautious mother with Gabe and the dolphins, and I know for certain you will maintain that same standard with the twins when they arrive. My deepest wish, however, is that you would employ that same level of regard for your personal safety. You are not invincible. Bad things sometimes happen to good people. Molly didn't deserve to be murdered. You should never have had a gun pointed at your head. And Jack should still be with all of us, enjoying his wife and his role at the dorm."

Brian paused for a moment after that last thought and reached across the table for Chloe's hand before continuing his passionate plea, "Misfortune knows no boundaries, and sometimes, it creeps up on us when we least expect it. Be careful, Chloe. You are my angel here on Earth, and I want to share a long, wonderful journey together raising a beautiful family. It was a God moment that I was there the last time when Shannon was threatening your life, but we can't count on that. I wish I could protect you always-"

"It's okay, Brian, please trust me. Things are different now. I'm pregnant, and I was truly scared having that gun held to my head. I don't want that ever to happen again."

"Me either. I'm so grateful that God, with the help of Grace, delivered me to you in time that evening, Dolphin Girl."

"Each time I pray for God's protection from evil, without fail, God provides," Chloe said.

"Your faith is commendable. The twins will be blessed to receive such a strong spiritual foundation from their mother."

"It has guided me through all of my ups and downs, and my hope is that it will fulfill them in the same way. At the very least, they will have the information and subsequently the opportunity to choose for themselves."

"Spoken like a true teacher. Always provide the knowledge, and then let the children decide for themselves," Brian said, squeezing Chloe's hands.

"Let's not get too ahead of ourselves," Chloe said and laughed. "The babies aren't even here yet! And while I'm thoroughly enjoying having dinner with my husband, my friends will soon be expecting me to join them for dessert at Sprinkles. We're meeting tonight to discuss plans for Jack's memorial service. If we can put together an outline, then Rose can simply make suggestions and give her approval. We're hoping to pull it all together so that she doesn't have too many worries. She plans to write the eulogy, of course, and that will be difficult enough for her to deliver on Sunday in front of what I am sure will be a large crowd."

"Once you and the other ladies have a plan, just let me know what I can do to help bring it all together."

"Thanks, Sweetie. You can count on us needing your assistance. It's going to take all of us chipping in, so that we can honor Jack in the way he truly deserves."

"No worries, Dolphin Girl, Jack will know and feel how much he was loved. Having the service amongst the dolphins and other animals at Dolphin Connection will certainly make him smile when he looks down."

"That is something we should each know from our family and friends while we're here on our Earth, in addition to when we cross to the other side to be with God. The deep feelings of love shared between Jack and Rose were always apparent, which makes me wonder why I can't shake this feeling that she is carrying with her some sort of regret," Chloe said, trying to encourage Brian to keep up with his doubts where Rose was concerned as she certainly was, although she wasn't sharing her reasons why.

"Keen observation, Dolphin Girl. Rose is definitely holding something just below the surface. For now, let's not press her. Once Jack's service is held, it will be more appropriate to push for answers. Out of respect for both of them, this time, it can wait," Brian said, obviously, from the look on his face, wishing he didn't think that way and could get on with exploring his suspicions.

"Most definitely - I couldn't agree with you more," Chloe said, letting out a huge sigh, which she hoped didn't reveal just how relieved she was that he was also backing off until after the funeral. "Now, before the ladies think I forgot about our dessert date, let me tell you how much I love you, inside and out!"

"Or they may think you've gone into labor!"

"Don't even put that thought out there into the energy field! I'm not ready yet. I'm still enjoying being pregnant! The day these babies decide to arrive, our life is going to explode with activity!"

"I'm tired just thinking about it! It will be a blast, though, that's for sure," Brian said, leaning in gently and kissing Chloe's cheek.

"Certainly, there isn't anyone else I'd rather be setting off on this new adventure with than you! Thank you for making all my dreams come true, Detective White."

"You've woken me up to dreams I didn't even know I had, Dolphin Girl. It's much more fun to be a "dream team" than it is to be a lonely dreamer."

"Look who's the wordsmith tonight! Couldn't have said it better myself!"

Chloe giggled and just knew she was glowing from the inside out.

Brian embraced her and carefully led her out of the restaurant so that he could deliver her on time to her awaiting friends.

Chapter 19

Bailey, Jenna and Eliza were already at the counter placing their orders when Chloe arrived at Sprinkles.

There were so many delicious choices on the menu, it was a challenge to order just one thing. Even though pregnant with twins, Chloe didn't think it was appropriate to order more than one dessert. She decided on a double-scoop sundae with her favorite flavors – mint chocolate chip and black raspberry – hot fudge, whipped cream and mini M&M's.

While they were all enjoying their delectable ice cream creations, Chloe filled in her friends on what she knew about the funeral plans so far. "All the food for the service on Sunday will be coming from Bagels on Broadway. Ann and Greg have decided to donate everything in order to honor Jack's memory. So, that is one thing we can cross off our list."

"What a kind gesture and a financial relief for Rose," Jenna offered. "What remains on the list for the four of us to tackle?"

"The list is short, but it will take some serious work on our part to achieve in two days, especially since Brina is still away at her training conference. Theresa told me earlier that she had ordered 100 chairs to be arranged in front of the underwater viewing area. That leaves us with flowers, music, programs and an honorary item," Chloe explained.

"What do you mean by an 'honorary item'?" Eliza asked.

"Something to send everyone home with that will remind them of Jack. The last couple of mornings, I've been writing down bits and pieces of a poem, which I'll print out. Each of the dolphins could add a touch of their artistic painting around the border, and we could make copies. Maybe laminate it, if there is time tomorrow, so everyone can pin it up at home as a reminder of Jack."

"Love that idea, Chloe!" Bailey exclaimed. "If you would like to work on that item, I'd be happy to take care of the music. I can almost guarantee the trio from my church would be happy to provide some suitable songs, and maybe I'll even have the opportunity to join in."

"They are wonderful. I heard them when I attended services with you, and having you accompany them on the keyboard would be a special treat. Three or four songs should fit the timing. Let me know how much of our budget we should put aside to pay them. Theresa is planning to cover all of the expenses," Chloe said, so grateful for her supportive friends.

"That leaves the flowers and the programs," Eliza noted. "Since I love writing, how about I design and print the programs, and you order the flowers, Jenna?" Eliza suggested.

"Perfect," Jenna agreed. "Flowers are just right for me. That is a challenge I'm up to, and I happen to know Jack's favorite flower was the hibiscus. That's why there are so many of them lining the path from the facility to the dorm!"

"Together, we are going to create a service that respectfully honors Jack's life, which will include a twist of 'dolphinality,' of course!" Chloe said, shaking off goosebumps as she felt Jack in her heart approving their plans.

"Are the dolphins going to be a part of the service?" Bailey asked.

"Yes. Evidently, Theresa has something special planned for the end of the service which should be truly magical. Rose is finishing up the draft for the programs tonight, Eliza. You should be able to pick it up from her in the morning," Chloe said, filling in the last of the details.

"It is so perfect to have the newest member of our dolphin family arrive in time for the service on Sunday. When Theresa's letter was circulated this afternoon, there was a collective cheer among all the staff. Nix has no idea how much love is in store for him during his stay at Dolphin Connection," Jenna interjected.

"Agreed! And on another note, does Rose plan on having a minister run the service?" Bailey asked.

"Since she and Jack were more spiritual than religious, Rose decided not to formalize the service with a minister. She asked me to guide things along from the Welcoming to the Closing. It will certainly be an emotional experience, but I was honored to say yes," Chloe stated.

"That role totally fits you," Eliza assured Chloe. "You always display grace under pressure."

The other two trainers nodded in agreement.

"Thank you for your belief in me, ladies," Chloe said, so appreciating their support. "I am going to need some of my sister's composure and strength to hold myself together throughout this experience. She is the 'graceful' one, that's for sure. Jack and I hit it off my first day on the job at Dolphin Connection. His warm, uplifting spirit and wonderful sense of humor drew me in right from the beginning. This is going to be really hard for me to do."

"You've got this, Chloe," Jenna reaffirmed as she reached over and gave Chloe a warm hug. "By the way, how is Rose holding up? She must still be in a state of shock."

"Most definitely!" Chloe agreed. "She has pushed herself to hold things together until the service is held. The injured collared dove she is nursing back to health has kept her busy, which is a positive thing."

"The what?" Bailey interrupted.

"When I was walking up the path of the dorm this morning, I found a baby collared dove, and Rose and I took it over to see Dr. Shelley, and she said it would need some tender loving care before it could be released. We all agreed it would be a Godsend for Rose right now, so we stopped at the store for some supplies and Brian set up everything when we got back to the dorm. It felt like Jack sent Rose a little guardian angel in the guise of a young collared dove she named Fuzzy."

"That is amazing!" All three trainers said.

"Yes, this sweet little fuzz-ball seems to be just what the doctor ordered," Chloe agreed. "In the midst of the grief, Fuzzy has given Rose somewhere to pour her heart out. She seems to be holding up the better for it. Although, something about Jack's death does seem to be nagging at her."

Before she could stop herself, these last words had slipped out. *Darn it!* Sometimes, her mouth worked faster than her brain.

"Do you think she knows something more than what she is letting on about what happened the other night?" Eliza asked.

"I'm not sure what it's all about," Chloe said, "but, I do intend to figure it out once the service is over. Until then, I promised Brian I'd let it go."

"Brian actually agreed to let you investigate?" Bailey asked, surprise present in her voice and on the look on her face.

"Well, technically, I agreed to let it go completely, but what I really meant was that I'd let it go until Monday," Chloe explained to her friends, wishing she had kept her big mouth shut for once.

"Chloe!" They all exclaimed together.

Quickly getting up from the table, gathering the garbage and heading to the trash can, Chloe removed herself from the conversation and called over her shoulder to her friends, "Well, it looks like that's a wrap! Let's all FaceTime to catch-up on our progress tomorrow evening, if we don't cross paths at the facility during the day."

"Chloe!" They all chanted again.

When Chloe stopped and looked back, they were all three shaking their heads as they followed her out the door of the café.

One of them whispered loud enough that Chloe could hear her that Brian wasn't going to be happy if she got involved in another one of his cases, especially in her condition.

Chloe, pretending not to hear what she knew was a correct statement, waved over her shoulder as she was getting into her car.

"Enjoy your evening, everyone!" She called out and closed the door before her friends could chide her once more.

Chapter 20

The next couple of days flew by as Chloe and each of her friends accomplished their responsibilities for the funeral service. From breakfast with Rose on Friday, to helping welcome Nix that morning, Chloe had maintained a steady pace of productivity.

Saturday evening, when her FaceTime ringer alerted her of a group call from her friends, Chloe was ready to go with her notes. Busy all day creating something she felt proud of to distribute at Jack's service the next day, she was more than prepared for the meeting.

"How's everybody doing tonight?" She asked as the others came into view on her screen. "Any problems getting your assignments for tomorrow accomplished?"

"The flowers will be delivered to Dolphin Connection first thing in the morning," Jenna chimed in. "And they are sure to be stunning – the shop owner and I decided on a beautiful tropical theme that includes hibiscus, birds of paradise and gardenias."

"Three of Jack's favorites," Chloe noted. "Thanks for getting that scheduled, Jenna."

"Anything I can do to let Rose know we're there for her, I'm glad to do it," replied Jenna. "It just doesn't seem possible that Jack is gone, though. This week started off so wonderfully with the celebration of the baby shower at the dorm and then quickly turned into a nightmare. It just doesn't make sense."

"Not at all," Bailey and the others agreed. "Today, when I was going over the music for the service with the trio from church, the reality of the situation overwhelmed me. At the party just the other night, Jack and I were bonding over our love of great 80's music, and now I'm choosing songs for his memorial service. Doesn't seem possible that he's gone-"

"Or that anyone would want to hurt him," Eliza interrupted. "Working on the memorial programs all day gave me lots of time to think. And for the life of me, I can't come up with anyone who'd want to hurt Jack."

"Maybe it was a freak accident," Jenna offered.

"That seems highly unlikely at this point," Chloe shared. "The autopsy seems to point in the direction of this being an intentional death. I'm not at liberty to share the details, but it definitely suggests foul play rather than an accidental fall. Hopefully, we will be able to get to the bottom of things quickly and find closure for Rose."

"We?" Bailey questioned.

"I meant Brian," Chloe quickly corrected herself, probably not quickly enough.

"Be careful, Chloe. Really careful this time. Your due date is around the corner, and you don't want to have any unnecessary complications at this delicate point in your pregnancy," Bailey offered, her voice tinged with loving concern.

"That's very true," Jenna agreed. "My cousin spent the last three months of her twin pregnancy in the hospital, and it was brutal. She was only allowed to get up to go to the restroom, and she didn't step outside into fresh air the whole time. Believe me, you don't want to end up lying in a hospital bed for the next three weeks. It's no fun, at all. I visited my cousin frequently, and she was miserable."

"I'm not going to do anything rash, and I'm certainly not going to end up in the hospital until these babies are actually ready to be born. If I casually come by information that will be helpful to the case, I'll certainly mention it to Brian. What I will not do is get actively involved in the case. Does that sound satisfactory to my pod of worriers?" Chloe sarcastically asked her beloved friends.

"We guess!" The ladies chimed in, one-by-one.

"Though, I'm not sure you can actually keep yourself from getting involved, Dolphin Girl!" Jenna said.

"That's true," Eliza agreed. "Somehow or another, the action always finds you!"

As her friends were laughing and shaking their heads, Chloe jumped a little and let out a small shriek which brought their attention back to the present.

"I believe these babies have a sense of humor because they are bouncing all over the place as if they are agreeing with the three of you," Chloe explained as she shook her head.

"We are their aunties," Bailey reminded her. And then continued, "It's like we're graduating from being a juvenile pod and becoming a maternity pod. The dolphins would be so proud of us!"

"They'll only be proud if we master this new way of life as smoothly as they do each time a calf or calves are born," Chloe said with a big grin on her face.

"They handle it with grace, that's for sure," Bailey said, as Jenna and Eliza nodded their heads in agreement.

"Just like my Grace," Chloe interjected. "She has made motherhood seem like a walk in the park. Compared to her, I hope I don't appear to be a bumbling fool."

"You've got this, Chloe!" Bailey said.

But suddenly, Chloe wasn't so sure.

"Grace does an amazing job, but you'll have your own style. An approach that works for you and Brian and your lifestyle together," Jenna reassured her.

"The truth is that these babies will lead a unique life. They may be the youngest ones yet to be introduced to dolphins!" Chloe exclaimed, feeling much better with the help of her friends' love and support.

"Your stomach is bouncing again, Chloe," Eliza pointed out. "It appears that your feisty twins can't wait for their first meet-and-greet with Kali, Emma, Alexa and Sophie, since they will certainly be their very first dolphin encounter."

"You've got that right on both fronts!" Chloe agreed excitedly. "That day will be a dream come true. In the meantime, I believe it would be helpful for me to have some dinner. These babies are incredibly active! It feels like they're doing somersaults, even though the doctor said there's not enough room for them to move around at this advanced state of the pregnancy."

"Doctors don't know everything!" Eliza piped up. "Those twins will surprise all of us with what they can do – I'm sure of it!"

"Amen to that!" Jenna offered, as barking dogs at her house contributed a background soundtrack.

"Sounds like it's dinnertime at your house too, Jenna," Chloe said. "Thanks a bunch for everything, ladies. You are all my saving graces!"

"No worries," her faithful friends replied.

"How about we meet in my office at 9 AM?" Chloe asked.

Everyone nodded in agreement, said their goodbyes and almost simultaneously ended their FaceTime calls.

Chloe slowly flipped down the screen on her laptop, feeling so much gratitude for these amazing people she was lucky to call friends.

Even as she focused her mind on the awesomeness of Bailey, Jenna and Eliza, her thoughts crept back to Jack and the way he had died.

The memorial service the next day to honor his life was going to be meaningful and heartfelt, but something nagged at Chloe, nonetheless.

There was no honor in letting Jack's murderer think he or she had gotten away with ending the life of such a valuable human being. The only way Chloe would feel like she was really honoring Jack would be to find out what really happened to him and make sure that the responsible party was brought to justice.

Further investigation would have to wait until Monday, though. Once the memorial service was respectfully carried out, then Chloe would place her imaginary detective's cap back on her head.

Chapter 21

Chloe couldn't tell if she was dreaming or not, but she suddenly found herself at the memorial service for Jack.

She'd started out sleeping peacefully that night, curled up with Brian and Gabe by her side.

So, this had to be a dream, didn't it, she wondered.

Jack was there, standing before her with a message, and it all felt so very real…as if he were alive again…

Everything was beautiful – the flowers, the music, the dolphins. There wasn't an empty seat. Though someone was missing.

Where was Rose?

A figure resembling Jack stood next to Chloe and kept trying to lead her away from the center of activity.

She stood frozen, despite the urging of the presence that stood next to her. And nothing was making sense. How could she be standing in the back, overlooking the scene, while she was also up front welcoming everyone to the service. It was impossible for her to be in two places at the same time, wasn't it?

Chloe was foggy and confused, but she kept feeling a tug to look around and take in the details. When she scanned the scene, her eyes rested on something strange.

Off to the side, Rose was talking to a man Chloe had never seen before. The man had his hands firmly planted on Rose's wrists and wasn't letting her move. As she struggled to break free, there were tears in her eyes.

Finished with her welcome to the fellow mourners, Chloe stepped around the corner and came face-to-face with Rose and this unidentified stranger. He ran away, while Rose shot Chloe a desperate look that pleaded for her to keep her mouth shut.

While Chloe stood frozen in disbelief, Rose took the opportunity to slip away and take her place before the guests. Before Chloe had even processed what had happened, Rose had already started her eulogy for her beloved husband.

The Chloe who was overlooking the scene from the back of the service kept her focus on the man who was quietly slipping out of the facility unnoticed.

All eyes were on Rose, while he went on his merry way. Dressed like everyone else for the memorial, there was no reason for anyone to find him out of the ordinary.

The chills shooting up Chloe's spine made her aware that he was anything but.

As she felt herself coming to, realizing it had all been just a dream, she heard the male voice next to her, that sounded just like Jack, repeat over and over, "Be very careful. He's trouble."

Suddenly, Chloe's eyes were open wide, and Gabe was standing over her with a startled look.

"That was different," she murmured, trying not to wake Brian who was fortunately a sound sleeper.

With much effort, she clumsily heaved her swollen body out of bed and trudged to the bathroom. She splashed her face with water and looked in the mirror.

Seeing her startled and very unsettled reflection, she decided to keep her dream and message to herself for now. There was need to alarm or upset anyone else on the day of Jack's service. She decided to quietly slip back into bed, so as not to alarm Brian, and get a little more rest.

Chapter 22

When morning came, Chloe stayed in bed a little longer than usual, unable to grasp that the day ahead would be spent honoring one of her dearest friends. It just didn't seem possible that Jack was gone – his larger-than-life spirit taken from this world in such a horrific way.

Chloe sighed and melted into the warm embrace Brian offered her with outstretched arms. There were no words needed between them. Brian knew this day was going to be incredibly difficult for her, and, as always, he supported her in loving ways like this.

"I'll be okay," Chloe assured him as she reluctantly pushed back from his embrace, knowing she had to get ready to go.

"Take it one moment at a time and know that I'll be right there to support you. All day long, no exceptions."

The possibility of him being pulled away onto a case consistently loomed large in her mind, and she sure hoped one wouldn't take him from her today. She appreciated his energy willing it not to be so as well.

"There's always a chance they'll need you, Brian. You know that. It's part of your job, and I'm okay with that," she said, trying to comfort him as much as herself with the reality of their life. "It's not my first choice, but I know it's a sacrifice that's worth making. You've helped so many people throughout your career. If you're called in today, go. I'll handle things at the service. I'm strong in ways you sometimes forget. I was on my own for a long time before we met. I'd prefer to have you there today as we reflect on Jack's life, but my legs will hold me up, and I'll still feel your support even if you can't be there physically the whole time."

"Why are you so focused on me being called in today, Dolphin Girl? There don't seem to be any foreseeable problems on the horizon, and today is Sunday, the one day I struggle to keep sacred. Are you feeling uneasy about something?" Brian asked.

"I'm just experiencing an undercurrent of unsettledness, like a situation may arise for you later in the day, and I wanted you to know ahead of time that I'm fine with it," she said, knowing her dreams were never just dreams, entirely.

"Oh boy! That's not good. I'm not picking up on that vibe, at all. But, then again, I usually don't, do I? I guess we'll just have to wait and see whose gut has it right!" Brian joked.

"Really, you're betting against a pregnant woman? My senses are heightened now beyond measure. I've never experienced anything like it before in my life," Chloe said, knowing she was spot on, once again.

"Very true. Okay…I'm taking my bet off the table. But you have an unfair advantage!" Brian said and chuckled.

"Time is flying by! We need to stop chatting and start driving our cars over to Dolphin Connection. I want to be early and make sure we've got everything arranged ahead of time."

"I'll take Gabe out for a short walk while you get dressed and have some breakfast."

"Thanks, Sweetie. I definitely need to eat something before we leave. My nerves are on edge, and the twins are kicking like crazy ever since I woke up. And they're not going to calm down unless I fill this ever-growing tummy of mine," Chloe said.

She quickly made herself some scrambled eggs, bacon and lightly-buttered, wheat toast. She knew the protein from the eggs was important to help curb her never-ending hunger. While she had enjoyed eating for three these last eight months, she looked forward to getting back in shape once the babies were born.

She'd have to continue to watch her diet while she was nursing, too, so taking off the baby weight would hopefully come relatively easily. While consistent exercise and juggling her time and schedule between simultaneously caring for her newborn babies and continuing to work for Dolphin Connection would be tricky, Chloe believed she was up to the challenge. And that challenge should result in plenty of lost pounds.

Realizing she was daydreaming, again, she quickly washed her plate and tumbler just moments before Brian and Gabe returned. She noticed the hibiscus flowers decorating the tumbler and smiled, remembering that Jack had given her this gift because they shared a love of Tervis and hibiscus.

It was no coincidence Jack was showing himself again, even if only symbolically this time. Evidently, he really wanted her to be aware and take notice of everything today.

Her phone buzzing brought her back into the present moment, and she quickly scrolled through the album of pictures with anecdotes Grace had sent.

She had received updates the past several mornings and felt as if she were enjoying the trip with Grace, Matt and the kids, just from a distance. She sent Grace a quick message and received prayer hands, dolphin and heart emojis accompanied by the simple statement, "I'll be there with you in my heart – Love, Grace."

And with those words from her twin, Chloe knew she would make it gracefully through the day.

Once they arrived at Dolphin Connection, it was all business.

Brian set to work on the physical tasks of unloading everything from the cars and bringing it all to the gathering area. Fortunately, the tables and chairs had been delivered the night before and were in great order, so he didn't have to mess with those.

Ann and Greg, dependable as ever, already had tablecloths in place and were finishing up arranging a beautiful brunch spread that would be sure to please all in attendance.

The two couples warmly greeted one another and then immediately went back to their jobs. There was no time for chitter chatter.

The morning passed by quickly, as each person contributing to the service arrived with their items and effortlessly joined the flow of the set-up already in progress. With time to spare, Dolphin Connection had been transformed into a wonderful and peaceful setting for the memorial.

While a sad event, at least it would take place in beautiful surroundings, and there was little chance the dolphins would keep their distance. They had quietly spied all morning as their human counterparts scurried around, curious to understand what the break from the normal routine of the facility meant for them.

They were to be a special part of the service, of course, but for them, it would be like a normal training session.

As 11 AM rolled closer, guests steadily streamed in and took their seats. Fortunately, the pavilion where the service was being held was still in the shade at this time of the day, so everyone would have some protection from the intensity of the Florida sun.

The scene looked eerily similar to the one staged in Chloe's dream the night before, which was not helping her get through it, at all.

As Chloe finished her warm and gracious welcome, Theresa sent the maternity pod – Cali, Emma, Alexa and Sophie – out for a series of front dives. What Theresa had planned for the girls was fitting as each one had held a very special place in Jack's heart.

Jack had been truly in awe of the fact that there had been twin dolphins born at the facility because it was such a rarity. Ever since Alexa and Sophie had made their grand entrance into the world the year before, he had studied the members of the maternity pod closely, and he planned to work with Chloe on creating an educational seminar about his observations, highlighting the ways in which the twin dolphins learned in unique ways that sometimes differed from singleton dolphins.

Chloe discreetly slipped from her place in front of the guests to make space for Rose to deliver her eulogy. Rose, however, was nowhere in sight.

Chloe glanced around the corner of a beautiful Bird of Paradise which had been placed there strategically by the florists and spotted Rose a stone's throw away talking to a man who appeared to be her contemporary in age. She wasn't alarmed at first, until she noticed the gentleman, if you could call him that, holding Rose firmly at her wrists as she struggled to get away.

"Rose, it's time for the eulogy. Is everything okay?" Chloe called out to her in as loud a whisper as she could, so as not to be overheard by the guests.

Fortunately, everyone was mesmerized and completely distracted by the grace and beauty of the four most magnificent female dolphins in the world.

When the entangled couple heard Chloe's voice, they were both startled, and the man quickly released his grip on Rose's wrists. In a flash, he dodged for cover, and Rose sped past Chloe to appear to seamlessly take her place in front of the guests.

Nobody seemed to realize there had been any sort of a disturbance. As they turned their attention away from the dolphins, who were finished with their flips, and back to the service in progress, a composed Rose was in place, ready to greet them.

Rose began to talk easily about the man with whom she shared so many special years of her life, the shakiness in her voice seeming to be completely normal, considering the fact that her husband had so suddenly and unexpectantly reached the end of his life.

Chloe, for her part, however, was shaken to her core.

While everyone else focused on Rose and supported her with their love and warmth, Chloe stood in shock and disbelief at what had happened in front of her eyes, only moments before.

The scene matched her dream with alarming detail and accuracy. She knew at once that there had been significant meaning behind that dream, and that it was probably more of a spiritual encounter with Jack than a plain ol' dream.

Jack had instructed her to keep watch over this suspicious man, and that was exactly what she was going to do.

Forcing her feet to move from the place where they were presently frozen, she rushed in the direction the man had gone. She looked everywhere, but the man had seemed to vanish.

Being that she needed to step back in as soon as Rose was finished, she couldn't go too far.

Rounding a corner that allowed her a view of the Visitor's Center and Restrooms, she saw someone trying to slip cautiously into the men's room.

Much to her dismay, as the stranger ducked through the door with the large blue dolphin on it, he glanced behind him, noticing Chloe staring in his direction.

She had hoped to stay invisible, but now felt threatened in a very unfortunate way.

There was no chance she could share her dream or real-life encounter with anyone while the service was in progress, but she knew that also meant her safety was now compromised.

And...she was now 100% sure Jack did not have an accident, he had been murdered, and it was highly likely she had just witnessed his murderer sneaking around at his memorial service.

Chloe would have to be careful not to be caught alone, though. Presently, that would not be difficult, as she scurried to move back to the heart of the service and embrace Rose as she finished her speech.

Her eulogy had been more like a familiar conversation with friends and family. Everyone in attendance knew Jack and Rose considered Dolphin Connection their family – the students who stayed at the dorm and the dolphins who graced the waters – the children they never had. They were devoted to each other, had been since they met after college, and devoted to the facility, to a fault.

When Bailey, accompanied by the members of her church trio, began to sing and play *Do You Believe in Magic?* by The Lovin' Spoonful, there wasn't a dry eye in the place. It was the song Rose and Jack had danced to at their wedding, and they had recently heard it performed in person while they were on vacation at Epcot's Flower and Garden Festival.

While Jack's presence was missed, it was hard not to believe in magic as the dolphins spun and swam across their lagoon in time with the music.

Many moments were magical throughout the service, as more songs were played, special stories were shared and meaningful poems decorated with dolphin paint splatters (which Chloe helped them accomplish the day before) were offered to all of the guests. The food supplied by Bagels on Broadway was completely devoured by the hungry mourners. For some reason, Chloe thought, grief always brings forth deep hunger.

Jack's kind spirit and generous heart had been acknowledged wholly and completely. The day couldn't have gone more perfectly. Other than the creep who Chloe spotted for a third time that day as everyone was packing up and leaving.

Rose was walking off the docks at the rear of the facility after visiting with Tango and Cash, two grey faces that claimed a very special place in Jack's heart because of their pair-bonded lifelong friendship, when out of the corner of her eye, Chloe noticed the same man from earlier.

He surprised Rose and tried to pull her off to the side, but he was unsuccessful. She slipped away and rushed back towards the staff members who were still breaking down the tables and chairs.

The man, whose physical features Chloe felt familiar with enough now to describe to a sketch artist, slithered towards the nearest exit.

As chills ran up and down her spine, she fought every urge in her body to sound the alarm and expose this uninvited person on the grounds of her beloved Dolphin Connection. It would bring conflict and drama to an otherwise perfect day, though, so she just couldn't do it. She'd promised herself that, for this one day, she'd keep her detective's cap off.

Though this man seemed incredibly suspect, he may very well not be responsible for Jack's death. Maybe he was someone Rose had an issue with, like a brother from whom she was estranged, and revealing his presence would be both embarrassing and unnecessary.

Chloe tried to convince herself that a logical scenario would end up being the case and attempted to shake the man's haunting image out of her mind.

She wasn't sure if she would confront Rose, or not.

She knew she should at least have Brian run a background check on Rose and her family and friends from the past before she started asking any questions, but that would prove hard to accomplish since she wasn't supposed to be involved in the case, at all.

Caught in the midst of a moral dilemma that had no easy answer, Chloe simultaneously got kicked from the inside by both of the babies and splashed from the outside by Rainbow, whose tail packed a powerful punch because of his size.

The incredibly large and exquisite dolphin soon popped his head out of the water and chirped, squeaked and whistled at his trainer. If only she could understand his message, her problems would be solved.

Dolphins were smarter than any humans on earth. Rainbow knew the answers Chloe sought, she was sure of it, and though she couldn't technically translate his message, his name alone reminded her all would be fine in the end. For after the storm, there is always a rainbow.

Chapter 23

"A penny for your thoughts," Theresa offered as she came around the corner and brought Chloe back to the real world.

"Oh, Theresa, there you are. The activity of the day clearly has me exhausted, and I got caught up in my thoughts," Chloe explained. "Thank you for everything you did to make this day so heartfelt."

"Being able to make a contribution is what got me through this difficult time," Theresa said. "My heart is shattered in pieces right now. Jack and Rose have been here since the beginning when Shannon, my Dad and I got started. Losing Shannon was hard enough. It didn't seem possible that we could have another tragedy amongst our close-knit family at Dolphin Connection."

Without hesitation, Chloe reached over and hugged her dear friend, pulling her into a warm embrace. From behind, she felt a familiar hand on her back and knew immediately it was her husband.

"Looks like it is getting more and more difficult for you to give your warm hugs, Dolphin Girl," Brian said and chuckled.

"Fortunately for you, Detective White, I have a wonderful sense of humor and find myself adorable in my dolphin-themed maternity attire. Some pregnant women may have found that joke offensive, but I was actually thinking the same thing to myself, so I can't really be upset with you."

"You can never stay upset with me because you know how much I love you and always will," Brian responded, hugging her himself.

"There isn't a greater truth than that," Theresa chimed in. "You two love birds are happier than ever. The love and respect you have for each other is admirable in so many ways."

"Thank you, Theresa," Chloe and Brian exclaimed together. Followed by their usual statement when they said the same exact thing at the same time. "Jinx, you owe me a Coke!"

"Thank you for the comic relief, you two," Theresa said. "I needed to laugh to relieve some of the tension that has built up inside of me today."

"Ladies, on a serious note, you two have pulled off something very special here today, and I know you must both be emotionally and physically depleted. Everything has been placed back where it belongs, so the facility should be ready to receive guests again when you re-open your doors tomorrow morning," Brian informed them.

"There are a few things I'd like to go over about the case, and I need to do so at the office, so I'm going to make a brief stop there before I head home," Brian said.

That announcement definitely brought Chloe's mood into a much more somber place.

"Have you discovered any new pieces of evidence or found a viable suspect?" Chloe eagerly questioned her husband.

"My comment was not an invitation for you to get involved in the case, Dolphin Girl," Brian said, the slightest bit of irritation in his voice.

"You can't blame me for my interest in this case, Brian," Chloe passionately reminded her other half. "This one is truly personal."

Evidently sensing her stress, Theresa reached over and rubbed Chloe's back.

"Chloe, Brian is simply looking out for your safety during this fragile stage of your pregnancy. Trust that he knows how much this one means to you and have faith that he will achieve justice for Jack," Theresa said, while continuing to rub Chloe's back.

"Couldn't have said it better myself," Brian said, smiling at Chloe.

Chloe took a moment's pause before she spoke.

"You're both right, and in my heart, I know that," she reassured them while thinking to herself she'd have to keep secret her knowledge of the suspicious man she witnessed both with Rose earlier that day and the night before in her dream vision with Jack.

Making a promise to stay quiet, like the one she'd made to Rose, was so not like her, and she knew it may not be in the best interest of the case, either.

Nothing short of the deep empathy she felt for Rose being widowed so unexpectantly could have continued pushing her to keep what she knew under the radar.

But today…today was the day of Jack's funeral. Everyone deserved a day to mourn completely and respectfully.

That said, one more day of silence was all she was willing to give her friend. One more day shouldn't make a difference. Well, Chloe sure hoped not.

"You're agreeing with us and not putting up a fight," Brian pointed out. "Now that makes me more nervous than normal. It's so unlike you, Dolphin Girl!"

"Maybe I'm just maturing as I'm preparing for motherhood," Chloe offered, not even convincing herself of that.

"Or maybe…you have some scheme up your sleeve and want to throw us off track," Brian retorted.

"Time out!" Theresa said and giggled. "This conversation is going in circles, and I'm getting dizzy! Go ahead, Brian. I'll keep an eye on your girl until she heads home," Theresa assured him.

"Just remember, she may not be as agile as usual, but that won't stop her. She'll slip away before you even know it," Brian warned.

"Enough, enough, Detective! Be on your way and trust your wife," Chloe urged as she kissed her hesitant husband and gently nudged him in the direction of the parking lot.

Brian acquiesced and started to walk briskly in the direction of his car.

At that same moment, Jenna, Bailey, Eliza and Brina, who had returned early from a conference to attend Jack's memorial service, rounded the corner and joined Chloe and Theresa.

"Group hug, everyone," Jenna suggested lovingly, and the ladies came together in one united embrace.

"From the bottom of my heart, thank you. This day was special from start to finish," Chloe shared with her close circle of girlfriends. "We each did our part and made this a significant event to honor our special friend, Jack."

"Yes, ladies, thank you for all of your hard work. You each went above and beyond," Theresa said.

"Your part with the dolphins blew everything else out of the water, Theresa," Eliza said.

Nix, the newest member of Dolphin Connection, who had arrived smoothly the morning before and was visible through the underwater viewing area, began creating bubble rings and swimming through them as if to affirm Eliza's statement.

"He is magnificent," Brina noted.

"The children in attendance today were fascinated by his 'bubble rings.' I believe he will make a great dolphin ambassador to our students," Theresa added.

"Jack would have loved Nix. As it was, his presence was palpable when the dolphins were interacting. Their flips and whistles elevated the energy of the crowd from sorrowful to spiritual," Chloe said.

Her comment drew them all in, and the six women brought the day to a close with a group hug to end all group hugs.

Each of the ladies quietly headed towards their respective belongings and readied themselves to leave the grounds.

Being as pregnant as she was, before heading out, Chloe decided to spend a few more moments with each of the dolphins. It had occurred to her that each time she saw them, it may be the last before the babies arrived, and she wanted to assure each wonderful grey face that she would return as soon as possible.

As she was giving hugs and kisses to the maternity pod – the group that most understood how her life would change when the twins arrived – she was startled by a hand on her shoulder.

Just as she was about to lose her balance, she caught herself, preventing what would have been a more than awkward entrance into the dolphins' lagoon.

"My apologies," Rose gushed as she helped Chloe to her feet. "I should have called out to let you know I was approaching."

"No worries, Rose. You've had a long day. I'm just grateful I didn't land in the water. That would have made a splash only the dolphins could rival," Chloe said and chuckled, as her belly rose and fell with her own amusement.

"It seemed crucial to explain to you what occurred this morning before I gave the eulogy. The man you saw me with is Jack's estranged brother. He's been in and out of jail for longer than I can remember, and Jack had to set boundaries that kept him out of our lives. Jack went to the ends of the Earth to attempt to rehabilitate him, but after years of trying, he had to step back from the situation. Especially after his brother stole from him. When Travis, that's his name, showed up today, I knew immediately it would be Jack's wish for me to keep that boundary in place. My thought was confirmed when the first thing Travis asked about was whether or not Jack had left him any money in his will," Rose explained, wringing her hands.

"I'm relieved in a way," Chloe offered. "And for some reason, I had the suspicious feeling there was an estranged family member in the mix," Chloe continued. "Please be careful, Rose, even though Travis is family, he may still be dangerous if he is desperate enough for drug money."

"Travis may be a dirtbag, but he's never hurt me in any way, shape or form. Please let this go and keep it between us, Chloe," Rose requested. "It would be embarrassing to Jack to share this situation, and I know you wouldn't want to disrespect him in death."

"I'd never do that," Chloe exclaimed, feeling rather hurt by the insinuation of betrayal. "I'm just concerned for your safety, Rose!"

"You have a history of sticking your nose where it doesn't belong," Rose pointed out.

Chloe was well aware of that fact before her friend made her feel badly about it.

"No worries, I'll keep my nose right where it belongs this time around," Chloe retorted in a sharp tone.

Due to the rough day they'd had, though, she quickly softened her voice and attempted to help ease each of them out of the uncomfortable moment.

"This has been a rough week for us all, Rose, most especially for you," Chloe said, trying to ease their discord.

"And it wasn't just Travis who showed up, Jack's high school flame was the pretty red-head in the front row. She had every right to be there, but her decision to show up caught me off guard," explained a clearly rattled Rose. "She and Jack had spoken recently, completely in a plutonic fashion, but it made me uncomfortable, and so he immediately stopped their communication in all forms."

"Oh goodness! I'm so sorry she came today, how horrible," Chloe offered with complete understanding from one woman to another. "Let's just hug this out and say goodnight, okay?"

Rose nodded in agreement, and the two embraced briefly before they each went their separate ways.

"I'm sorry to run, but I've been worried about Fuzzy being alone all day," Rose called over her shoulder.

"No worries, please give him my love," Chloe called out.

Chloe drove home in silence, not even the radio able to keep her from the troubling thoughts she just couldn't escape. She felt filled with remorse over upsetting Rose on such a difficult day.

When she arrived home, she sobbed in the loving warmth of Gabe. He held no judgment, simply offering her unconditional love and empathy.

When Brian arrived home, Chloe had cleaned up her face so she wouldn't make him suspicious. When he filled her in on the background check he had completed on Jack's family and friends, he mentioned an estranged brother with a drug issue, and Chloe almost fell off her chair.

Rose had been telling the truth.

Brian went on to mention that he compared the partial print lifted from the ice pick with Travis's DNA profile on the Combined DNA Index System (CODIS), but there was no match, nor was there a match to anyone else. That meant the person who did kill Jack had no previous record.

Chloe now knew that her first stop in the morning would be at the dorm. She needed to apologize to Rose. Knowing she had upset her grieving friend, she wouldn't sleep well until she'd made sure Rose knew how sorry she was.

Chapter 24

Set on seeing Rose and apologizing for her behavior the previous evening, the dawn of the new day came early for Chloe.

She found it hard to believe that Rose's story matched the information uncovered by Brian, though that seemed to be the truth, so she'd have to come to terms with it. Regardless, she remained confused by the message of her dream vision with Jack and knew she would have to dig further to understand his symbolic references.

Unfortunately, she'd gotten it wrong up to this point.

As she'd mentioned to Rose when they'd had their heated conversation, Chloe was relieved in a way that the man who had Rose on edge was simply a troubled brother of Jack's. The last thing she wanted was for Rose to have any connection whatsoever to what happened to Jack – accident or murder.

Rose treated Chloe as she would have her own daughter, and Chloe knew how important it was to have such an extraordinary woman as Rose having her back during this period of change in her life. She would be like a grandmother to the twins, which was a huge relief since Chloe and Grace's own mother had made it distinctly clear that she was too busy with her own travels to be there for either one of them.

Grace was fortunate to have Matt's mother, and Chloe knew Brian's mother would be an amazing grandma, though having Rose right on the grounds of Dolphin Connection would be an amazing blessing.

Chloe wanted to make things right with Rose immediately, if not sooner, and picked up her pregnant pace, so that she would reach the dorm as soon as humanly possible.

Even in a rush, she was never too busy to pick up a plastic shopping bag, one of which she had just tripped over on the path. It drove her crazy to see these bags strewn where they could be ingested by or entangle animals. Sometimes, she would pull over while she was driving down the road to pick up bags; other times, she would clean them off the beach and out of the water. There was no way she was leaving one on the grounds of her sacred space, the facility grounds.

As Chloe paused and awkwardly tried to bend down to retrieve the plastic bag, a figure stepped out of the shadows and into her line of sight.

"Let me pick that up for you," the man who moved towards her demanded in a rather forceful tone.

"Okay, thank you for the help," Chloe said as she looked up from her crouched position and stared into the eyes of the man she had seen with Rose several times the day before.

"Travis?" Chloe asked.

The man looked at her with an inquisitive stare that immediately informed her that although Jack indeed had an estranged brother named Travis, as verified by Brian the night before, this man was clearly not him.

Rose had used Travis as a cover story!

"What are you talking about?" The man shouted in Chloe's face. "My name isn't Travis, and I'm not really interested in helping you clean up this bag. I could care less about your environmental concerns. You may be worried about this bag suffocating an animal, but what you should really be worried about is me using it to cut off your oxygen supply."

Chloe had no idea of the identity of the man who stood before her.

Both her mind and body froze in disbelief that she had put herself in mortal danger, once again.

The stranger moved closer to Chloe, causing her to stumble, but luckily, she caught herself. As he continued to close in, she took more steps backwards until she felt her feet enter the water, not surprising since it was only a few feet from the edge of the pathway.

"Stop!" The man, seething with anger, yelled. "I can't get this bag over your head if you are moving."

For once, Chloe's expanded tummy came in handy, making it more difficult for this crazed person to reach her head. As he made a lunge forward and succeeded in throwing his makeshift weapon over Chloe's head, she tripped over some pieces of coral rock and fell hard on her bottom in the compact sand. Fortunately, the water was shallow enough that her head and chest area remained above the surface.

"Doesn't look like it's your lucky day. Maybe if you weren't so nosey, you wouldn't have landed yourself in this position," the stranger continued as he tried to secure the bag he already had in place over Chloe's head.

Just in the nick of time, as he was about to completely cut off her air supply, wings of grace appeared in the frantic movements of Fuzzy. The brave bird flew directly into the midst of the altercation, announcing himself with a distinct dove call. With his beak, he pulled the trash bag off Chloe's head.

Chloe, meanwhile, used her arms to wrestle with her assailant.

Fuzzy, having the advantage of flight, took off with the bag flapping in the wind, into the outstretched arms of Rose who beckoned him from the bottom of the dorm steps.

"Chloe!" Rose shrieked in unison with Brian who was just coming around the corner of the building.

When Brian saw the scene in front of him, without hesitation, he ran into the water and tackled the madman who was attacking his wife. Within moments, he had him in handcuffs, holding him to the side with one hand, as he reached out and helped Chloe to her feet with the other.

Rose and Fuzzy were there, as well, which was fortunate because Chloe was shaking and gasping for air.

In the far distance, sirens could be heard approaching. The staff members at Dolphin Connection must have called 9-1-1 as soon as they heard the commotion, Chloe figured.

Brian and Rose helped Chloe to a nearby bench until help arrived.

"You should be ashamed of yourself, Adam," Rose yelled in the direction of the man handcuffed and curled in the fetal position on the ground nearby.

"Adam?" Chloe questioned, coming out of her shock, surprising both Rose and Brian. "I thought he was Jack's brother, Travis."

"Travis?" Brian responded. "That can't be Travis. He's in jail in Colorado on drug charges at the present time."

"You lied to me?" an injured Chloe asked her trusted friend, feeling her own crushing disappointment all over her face.

"I'm sorry, Chloe. This is all my fault," Rose apologized. "I was too embarrassed to tell you about Adam. He was my first love, back in high school, and when he contacted me on social media a few weeks ago that he was in the area and wanted to have lunch, curiosity got the best of me and I went. That one lunch ruined my life. Adam had been following me for years online and quickly became obsessed once we met in person again. I knew it was wrong the moment I sat down at the table the day we met up, but I was too ashamed to tell Jack what I'd done. It was just lunch, but it was behind Jack's back, and it was a betrayal of his trust. When Adam wouldn't leave me alone, it felt like there was nowhere to turn, and now Jack's dead and you're hurt, Chloe," Rose said in between sobs.

Filled with empathy, Chloe placed her personal pain aside for the moment and embraced her distraught friend.

"You could have told us all the truth, Rose. We would have helped you. We're your friends. We're here to assist you, not judge you," Chloe offered.

"And I could have done the same for you, Dolphin Girl, if you'd been forthcoming with me last night. I knew you were holding something back on me, but I let it go after such a draining day," Brian said, hurt heavy in his voice as he continued, "Never did I imagine you'd already have yourself in a predicament at the dawn of the very next day. It's a good thing I uncovered a string of serial calls to Rose from a burner phone as I was researching her phone records this morning and then proceeded directly over here to question her about it."

"I've learned my lesson this time, for real. I never want to be that scared again, especially for the lives of our babies," a worried Chloe assured her husband.

"And I've learned mine, too," Rose added.

"A husband always forgives his wife," Brian said, trying to comfort both of them with his words. "Whether he's right in front of her or watching over her from afar," he continued, gazing in Rose's direction.

A 'tweet' of agreement from Fuzzy confirmed his message.

"Thank you, Detective White. You are simply the best," Chloe expressed sincerely to the man she knew would always stand by her side.

Not a moment too soon, Police and EMS appeared around the corner. Brian briefly informed them of the situation with the man in handcuffs and quickly joined Chloe in the back of the waiting ambulance.

Epilogue

Merina Jacqueline and Aleta Rose were born sixteen minutes apart shortly after Chloe and Brian arrived at the hospital the morning Fuzzy came to the rescue. The commotion had set Chloe's body into labor, and the doctors agreed she was far enough along for the babies to make their way into the world.

The transition into parenthood was an easy one for the Dolphin Duo, and they threw themselves into being the best possible.

They loved their girls more than they thought imaginable. And Gabe loved them, too. He even shared September 12th as a birthday with them. When the date of the twins' birth was recorded, the proud parents looked at each other in amazement, realizing that with all the recent commotion, they had forgotten Gabe's birthday that morning. They couldn't be happier Gabe would officially be a 'furry triplet' to the twins!

Though she wasn't due back at work yet, Chloe often visited her human and dolphin family at the facility with the babies. As they saw her approaching with the stroller, the dolphins would screech in delight.

Merina and Aleta would be blessed with 'dolphin memories' from their very first days on Earth. The maternity pod appeared to take great pride in the adorable bundles of joy, swimming back and forth when Chloe would walk the twins up and down the path attempting to get them to sleep.

Nix, for his part, blew the most elaborate bubble rings when Chloe parked the carriage in front of the underwater viewing area. He loved to nod to each girl, acknowledging there wasn't just one addition, but two.

There were rumblings of hope that one of the female dolphins who had been paired with Nix may be pregnant. Fingers-crossed, a sweet new grey face would join the growing family in roughly fourteen months!

Chloe was enjoying some quiet time as she waited for everyone else to arrive at the dorm. Their home had seen a constant parade of family and friends since the birth of the twins, and it was nice to breathe in some solitude.

Grace, without a doubt, had helped Chloe the most. She was there to help her recover when she came home from the hospital and was the savior who had the twins on a schedule by the time she went home. The bond of the newborns brought back sacred memories for Chloe and Grace, twins to the core.

It was the most perfect Florida day, and Chloe soaked in the sunshine. When Rose spotted she and the little ones outside, she joined the happy trio with the ever-present Fuzzy on her shoulder.

The DA's Office, after much persuasion from a persistent Detective Brian White, had chosen not to press charges against Rose for Obstruction of Justice since she agreed to help them build their case against Adam Thomas. For now, Rose was still healing, pouring herself into Fuzzy's rehabilitation and hosting new classes of Dolphin Learners at the dorm. It was clear she would need some assistance, but no permanent arrangements had yet been made.

Theresa arrived with the trainers and other staff members from Dolphin Connection, as did Brian and other friends. They were all dedicating a dock at the dorm in honor of Jack. It seemed a wonderful tribute for a man who felt just as comfortable on the water as on land.

There was a long pier that led to a stationary dock with a thatched roof, a beautiful bench and a recycling bin with a special logo of Fuzzy on it.

Ever since the miraculous dove had saved Chloe's life, she had made it her personal mission to help people understand the importance of reducing, reusing and recycling. Theresa joined forces with her, and together, they not only banned the use of plastic bags at the facility, they helped make it a town-wide regulation, replacing the harmful plastic with reusable cloth bags proudly displaying the picture of a collared dove, who was also a local hero!

The pier and dock named for Jack would be a place where students and staff could retreat and be one with their surroundings. The wonderful idea to have this as Jack's legacy dropped into Chloe's head one morning after she had met up with him in her dreams.

She knew the plan was heaven sent.

As the minister who had come to bless the new structure finished her prayer, Fuzzy flew off Rose's shoulder, spreading his wings and circling over everyone present in what could clearly be recognized as a message of love and peace.

Even the twins, only a few months old at the time, reacted to the stunning flight.

Chloe, for one, sensed a spiritual presence in their midst, and when Brian squeezed her hand, she knew he felt the same thing.

Rose had a look of calm wash over her, so filled with God's light, it was clear to everyone in attendance.

This was their new normal at Dolphin Connection. A future in which Jack's spirit lived on, even though he no longer lived amongst them on Earth. He would guide and guard them from above, helping his wife, trusted friends and beloved dolphins have amazing new interactions, opportunities and relationships on the grounds of the place they all treasured – Dolphin Connection.

Jack kept the blessings flowing, and when each new one arrived, the recipient immediately knew from whom it had been sent.

THE END

Dolphin Fun Facts

- Dolphins belong to the Order Cetacea and the Family Delphinidae. The Orca, or killer whale, is the largest member of the family which is made up of over 30 different species.
- Many people around the world recognize the Atlantic Bottlenose Dolphin whose scientific name is Tursiops Truncatas. Bottlenose dolphins are found in many diverse types of waters across the world.
- Dolphins can be identified by their dorsal fin. Variations in the dorsal fin help us recognize an individual dolphin like the features of the face for a human. The tail flukes of a dolphin are also unique and can help a trainer identify a specific dolphin; similar to the handprints and footprints of people.
- The dorsal fin on a dolphin's back is used for stability. Their pectoral fins are for steering. Their tails provide great propulsion through the water and are enormously strong.
- Dolphins are marine mammals. They have belly buttons because they are connected by an umbilical cord in utero like humans. Dolphins breathe air through their blow hole located on top of their head, and they have whiskers around their rostrum when they are first born. A dolphin mother produces milk in order to nurse her calf.
- Dolphins can dive to great depths of up to 200 to 250 feet, though most tend to limit dives to shallow depths of roughly 10 feet hunting for

fish along the shorelines. A US Navy dolphin named Tuffy made an incredible dive over 900 feet!

- Dolphins usually stay underwater for an average of 8 to 10 minutes.
- Dolphins can swim at burst speeds of up to 25 to 30 mph, although it is more common for them to swim along at 7 to 8 mph.
- Dolphins only rest one half of their brain at a time when they sleep.
- The average life span of an Atlantic Bottlenose Dolphin in the wild is roughly 25 years. Some in human care have lived up to 40 or 50 years.
- Dolphins receive all of their water intake from the fish they eat. If a dolphin stops eating for any reason, the dolphin will become dehydrated quickly which can be very dangerous.
- Atlantic Bottlenose Dolphins use their 88 to100 conical shaped teeth to grab their prey. Then they swallow their fish whole in order to squeeze the water out.
- Dolphins eat their fish head first. This keeps the fin and spines of the fish folded back in such a way that they won't hurt the dolphin's throat.
- Dolphins eat various types of fish including herring, grouper, mackerel and sardines. At dolphin facilities and aquariums, dolphins eat restaurant-quality fish that is thoroughly checked and cleaned before it reaches a dolphin's mouth.
- It is important that dolphins in human care have "dolphin time" when there are no trainers or visitors around. This allows them to interact with each other without outside expectations.

- Dolphins live in social groups called pods. There are maternity pods which consist of mature females and calves, juvenile pods that are made up of males and females that are not sexually mature, and bachelor pods whose members are adult males. Some males become very close, similar to best friends for people. They are called pair-bonded. A pod can range from 2 to 30 members. It is an awe-inspiring sight to see dolphins in the wild hunting for fish in a pod and caring for their young.
- Research has shown that mature male and female dolphins do not live together as a family in the wild. Adult males seek out maternity pods to mate with adult females and then they quickly leave. Males practice intercourse on one another so that they will be efficient when they meet up with females and don't make themselves prey to sharks, etc. It is then solely the job of the mother to raise her calf with the help of the other females in the maternity pod.
- Dolphins normally give birth to one calf at a time. This way a pregnant female only develops a slight bulge in her belly area and stays streamlined in the water. Twin pregnancies are possible, though highly unlikely and result in challenging deliveries. Calves are born tail first (their tail is curled up) and when their head/blow hole emerges, the dolphin mother must nudge the calf to the surface quickly in order for it to take a breath.
- When a dolphin calf nurses, the calf will swim in the slipstream of the mother dolphin. The calf benefits by swimming very close in proximity to

the mother with the center of his body aligned with her tail. The calf moves along more quickly by riding the wake of the mother. From this location, the calf can insert its tongue, curled into a straw like shape, into the slit of the dolphin mother's mammary gland. Dolphin calves usually nurse for 1 to 3 years.

- Dolphins have a type of sonar called echolocation. This allows them to locate objects that are in their surroundings by sending out sound waves which bounce off the object and then return to the dolphin's melon (forehead) to relay information.

- Dolphins each have unique and interesting personalities. It's exciting when working with dolphins to get to know each one personally and discover their likes and dislikes.

- The signature whistle of a dolphin is like an individual name that affords dolphins the ability to recognize one another and be identified by humans.

- Dolphins have exceptional hearing even though they don't have external ears. Tiny pinholes located behind their eyes enable them to hear sounds over long distances.

- Dolphin vocalizations are extensive and can include whistles, clicks, chirps, pulsed sounds, squeaks and squeals. Dolphin training sessions can be quite a concert!

- Dolphins need both physical and intellectual stimulation on a daily basis. Training sessions allow dolphins to be challenged through exercise and problem-solving situations. If you visit a dolphin facility, you may see a dolphin recognize a shape or symbol that has been assigned to him or her. Through practice, the dolphin will identify and respond to his/her individual symbol.

- In general, Atlantic Bottlenose Dolphins are about 3 1/2 feet when they are born and weigh between 22 to 44 lbs. Mature adult males and females range in size and can grow up to 10 plus feet and weigh between 300 and 1,400 lbs.

- Though they may seem similar, most facilities use their own set of signals to work with their dolphins. That means a trainer who makes a move from one facility to another may have to learn new signals or use a different style of whistle to bridge. If you want to become a trainer, it is important that you work at a facility where you are comfortable with the overall policies and philosophical approach that pertain to the animals and the employees.

- Many trainers will conduct sessions with their dolphins from a platform or a floating dock that gets them very close to the dolphins, but not actually in the water with them. At other times, trainers will get right in the water with the dolphins to work on interactive behaviors like dorsal pulls that are sometimes used during a dolphin swim program or dolphin show. In-water time allows trainers to develop an even closer relationship with the dolphins in their own environment. It's important to be a very strong swimmer if you want to become a dolphin trainer, and it's also helpful to become scuba certified.

- In training sessions, positive behaviors are encouraged and acknowledged with a verbal and or physical interaction and a desired food source. This could be the whistle or the voice with dolphins, and, of course, fish. Further encouragement can include cheers and back rubs! Unwanted behavior is simply ignored.
- Dolphins have a complex systems of nerve endings which make their skin very sensitive to the touch. If you are fortunate enough to enjoy a dolphin swim at an accredited facility, you will probably spend some time giving the dolphins you interact with pectoral rubs and back rubs. It can be a truly magical moment when you first touch a dolphin!
- If you want to become a dolphin trainer, start researching the facilities that exist in Florida and across the country. Most facilities offer volunteer and internship programs to people of various ages. Several facilities also offer specialized classes so that you can further your knowledge of marine mammals in general and receive more hands-on interaction. Many dolphin trainers have a background in either biology or psychology and sometimes both. If it is your dream to work with dolphins, go for it!
- Joining and training to be a part of a dolphin stranding team through a local aquarium or organization can be a wonderful way to help marine life. Living in an area where dolphins are prevalent will mean more opportunities on a local level. Sometimes though, dolphins and other marine mammals, like manatees, need help far from their usual waters because of strange

weather patterns/storms, unhealthy water conditions, quickly changing tides or illness. The goal of rescue is always to rehabilitate and return an animal to his/her natural habitat. In cases in which an animal is not strong enough to return to the wild due to extensive injuries, health impairments or age, the corresponding government agency will select the appropriate marine life facility that can best meet the needs of the particular animal and give it a forever home.

• The National Oceanic and Atmospheric Administration (NOAA) recommends maintaining a minimum distance of 50 yards from any marine mammal in the wild. Feeding any marine mammals in the wild is illegal and can be extremely dangerous to the health of the animals. The Marine Mammal Protection of 1972 was signed into law on October 21, 1972 by President Richard Nixon and went into effect on December 21, 1972. In summary, the law forbids the collection of marine mammals and makes illegal the import, export and sale of marine mammals, their parts, or products made from their parts, within the United States. The enforcement of the regulations stated within the MMPA is an important part of the law. See the website of NOAA Fisheries for a detailed and complete description of the MMPA.

Related Sources

https://www.dolphins.org
https://www.nationalgeographic.com
http://www.noaa.gov

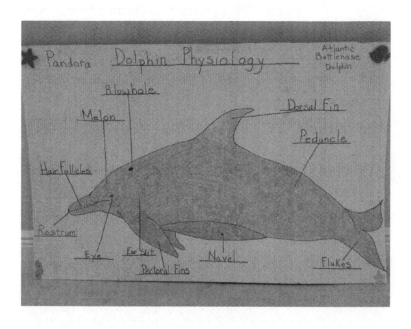

Collared Dove Fun Facts

1. Their scientific name is Streptopelia decaocto.
2. They are medium in size: an average length of 13 inches from tip of the beak to tip of the tail, have a wingspan of 19 to 22 inches and a weight that ranges between roughly 4 and 8 ounces.
3. They rank of "least concern" on the conservation status chart.
4. Collared doves have beautiful grey plumage that is slightly darker on their backs than their fronts. Both the wings and the tail have dark grey feathers with white markings at the ends. The front side of the wings boast beautiful light blue feathers. They have black beaks and a well-distinguished collar around the back of their neck. The red of their iris is stunning up close and the eye itself is surrounded by skin that is white or yellow in appearance. The short legs and talons of the collared dove are also red.
5. You cannot tell male and female doves apart just by looking at them.
6. Juveniles have a brown iris rather than red, and the collar on their neck is not well-developed.
7. Collared doves are native to Europe and Asia. In North America, they are considered an invasive species.
8. Eurasian collared doves made their way to North America when roughly a few dozen of them escaped from an animal facility in the Bahamas in 1974. They arrived in Florida first and then they spread all over the United States. Though

they can fly long distances, collared doves are not migratory.

9. Collared doves mate for life. Their nests are simple and made of sticks. The female lays two small white eggs in the nest which she and her mate have built together. They take turns sitting on the eggs which incubate for about three weeks in duration. If weather and food conditions are hospitable, collared doves can breed year round.

10. The average lifespan of a collared dove is 3 years. They can become very interactive when they live in human care. When in flight, the dove almost always makes a very distinct, loud sound for a few moments before landing.

Sources:
https://www.animalspot.net
https://www.discoverwildlife.com
https://www.wikipedia.org

~ 137 ~

About the Author

Tracey V. Williams resides in Lakewood Ranch, Florida
with her husband, twin daughters and Poochon. She has her
Masters in Teaching for Secondary Education and a
Graduate Certification in American Art from Sotheby's
Auction House. Over the years, Tracey has enjoyed
teaching Social Studies to middle school students, sharing
her love of dolphins with visitors at a marine mammal
facility, leading school groups on tours of Colonial
Williamsburg and having the opportunity to educate her
own children. Tracey's passion for writing began in
childhood and continues to grow each year.

For more information on the author and her books, please
visit www.traceyvwilliams.com and join her on:

Facebook: Tracey Williams
Pinterest: https://www.pinterest.com/traceyvwilliams/
Instagram: https://www.instagram.com/traceyvwilliams/

Books by Tracey V. Williams

Dolphin Trainer Mysteries (YA Romance/Mystery)
Dolphin Girl
Dolphin Duo
More Coming Soon!

Children's Picture Books
"GO BACK TO BED!"

Ninja the Penguin Series (Children's Chapter Books)
The Great Escape
Book 2 --- *Coming Soon!*

Tracey V. Williams
AUTHOR. TEACHER. MOM.

"I write books that I would
assign as a teacher and that I
would recommend as a mom."

~Tracey V. Williams

Made in the USA
Columbia, SC
14 March 2021